BY CRUMBS,
IT'S MINE!

BY JOHN AND PATRICIA BEATTY

Holdfast
King's Knight's Pawn
Master Rosalind
The Royal Dirk
Who Comes to King's Mountain?
Witch Dog
published by William Morrow and Company

At the Seven Stars
Campion Towers
A Donkey for the King
Pirate Royal
The Queen's Wizard
published by The Macmillan Company

BY PATRICIA BEATTY

The Bad Bell of San Salvador
Blue Stars Watching
Bonanza Girl
Hail Columbia
How Many Miles to Sundown
A Long Way to Whiskey Creek
Me, California Perkins
The Nickel-Plated Beauty
O the Red Rose Tree
The Queen's Own Grove
Red Rock Over the River
Rufus, Red Rufus
The Sea Pair
Squaw Dog
published by William Morrow and Company

Indian Canoe-maker
published by The Caxton Printers, Ltd.
The Lady from Black Hawk
published by McGraw-Hill Company

BY CRUMBS, IT'S MINE!

by Patricia Beatty

Fic
Bea

FRONTISPIECE BY LORING EUTEMEY

William Morrow and Company
New York   1976

Printed in the United States of America.
1 2 3 4 5   80 79 78 77 76

Library of Congress Cataloging in Publication Data

Beatty, Patricia.
  By crumbs, it's mine!

  SUMMARY: While stranded in the Arizona territory in the 1880's a thirteen-year-old girl finds herself the owner of a traveling hotel.
  [1. The West—Fiction. 2. Humorous stories] I. Title.
PZ7.B380544By   [Fic]   75-31574
ISBN 0-688-22062-2
ISBN 0-688-32062-7 lib. bdg.

FOR NETTIE FRISHMAN

CONTENTS

BY CRUMBS,
IT'S MINE!

1

MY ELEPHANT?

"Are you Miss Damaris Boyd, a terror on two feet?" the railroad conductor asked me. I was standing out in the train aisle stretching my arms, trying to forget our troubles.

"You know what my name is," I told him. He'd talked to me often enough around the organ at night, but I supposed he was being formal and polite, though what he'd said hadn't sounded very nice. "Why do you say that I'm 'a terror on two feet'?" I asked him.

"I didn't say it. It's written on this note for you." And then he gave me a piece of paper.

By crumbs, it *was* for me! My name was printed on the outside of it and under my name, sure enough, the words, "a terror on two feet." Because I was naturally curious about what the note said, I unfolded the paper. The message inside was written in fancy curlicue penmanship in lead pencil.

June 15, 1882 (1:00 p.m.)

Miss Damaris Boyd,

Being of sound health and wind and of
sounder mind than usual as of this moment,
I hereby sign over One Elephant, which goes
under the name of Nomad to your keeping and
ownership. You now own my elephant in all of
its parts, which are inclined to be white. I won
it long ago—as you can probably guess—by treading in my evil paths. May you enjoy it.

B. Benjamin, Esquire
Spar City
Arizona Territory, U.S.A.

An elephant! Mr. Benjamin wasn't only a mean
man, my mortal enemy, and a robber, but he had a
cruel sense of humor to boot. I got out of the aisle
and sat down next to my sister, Ann Viola. Oh, I
wanted badly to bite some nails right now. Not fingernails. Iron nails. Even though the seats of the
parlor car were covered with red plush, they were
hard as bricks, but all the same I plopped down so
hard that Ann Viola rose up into the air a little bit.

Mama and my brother William sat across from us.
She was perspiring in her linen duster, which she
always wore to keep train soot off her silk dress. She'd
been trying to tat some lace for nightgown trim, but
she'd given it up. It wasn't easy to do fancywork
while crying. My brother was looking out the train

window at what was Mexico not so many miles away to the south, according to other passengers. He hadn't even noticed that the conductor had given me a note. He was down at the mouth because he was still on the train, and he didn't want to be. As for Ann Viola, she was whining for a peppermint from Mama's purse, because she'd had to eat her lunch too fast back at Spar City and her stomach had begun to hurt her.

After Mama had given Ann Viola the peppermint, she sighed and asked me, "Damaris, what did the conductor give you just now? Is it a farewell note from your father?" She wiped her eyes with her handkerchief, though she'd stopped crying fifteen minutes back. Well, she wasn't the only lady on this train feeling unhappy, but that didn't comfort her much, I supposed. I knew it surely didn't comfort me.

I had to tell her, even though it was a silly and mean thing Mr. Benjamin had done. He had rubbed salt into our wounds. "No, it isn't from Papa. It's a note from Mr. Benjamin."

"Mr. Benjamin? That spotted hyena, that scalawag? He's the cause of our troubles. Your father would never have left us if it hadn't been for that man. Why did he write you a note, Damaris? Is he begging our pardon for what he did to us? Does he want to make amends?"

"I don't know what the note means. Maybe he only wants to make us feel worse. He wrote it in Spar City right after he and the other men heard the news. He left the train too. I don't understand him."

Mama snorted. It was a good sign. She was getting angry. Getting mad is a lot healthier for a person than sorrowing and moping. But she was paler than I'd ever seen her—so pale her nose freckles stood out more, and the heat made her reddish hair curlier. She moved around on her seat trying to get more comfortable and still be ladylike, which she set great store by. I knew how hard it must be for her to sit for hours at a time on a train seat wearing a bustle under her dress and duster.

Right now I was glad that I was only thirteen and didn't have to put my hair up in a headache-making knot or wear bustles or high-heeled boots. Mama looked exactly what she was—a nice lady from Saint Louis, Missouri, going for a trip. The trouble was, as I was beginning to see it, we were traveling in the wrong direction now that Papa had left us in Spar City. We were still headed west toward Leacock, Arizona Territory, when we should have been going east. Instead of heading for Uncle Owen Boyd at Leacock, we should be going to Massachusetts to Mama's relations, the Nesses, where we'd visited last year.

As I handed Mr. Benjamin's note to Mama, she said, reading my mind again, "Damaris, we are going the wrong way, you know. We should be heading to your Grandfather Ness in Pittsfield, Massachusetts, instead of going on to see another one of those bad Boyds."

At the mention of the "bad Boyds" William twitched. This time, though, she didn't mean him, but our father, Charles. According to Mama, who had once been Lucy Ness and had led a calm, gentle life on a farm, most of the men of the Saint Louis Boyds suffered from the same disease. She called it "get-rich-quick." It was a very dangerous ailment to have. I'd overheard Mama, who was interested in phrenology, talking to her sisters in Massachusetts last summer about the "curse of the Boyds with their bulging foreheads," and she had said she was glad that I was not a man and because of that wouldn't fall prey to the disease. Although I was a girl, I was the only one of the three of us who had inherited Papa's forehead, and mine didn't bulge very much at all. I didn't hold one bit with the idea that the bumps on your head showed what kind of person you were. I thought deep down that a head bulging where Papa's and mine did meant that we might have more brains inside our skulls than most other people. I look like him in other ways, too. I have his straight dark hair and brown eyes where William and Ann Viola are hazel-eyed with lightish curling hair and have Mama's Ness roundness.

I pondered Papa while Mama read Mr. Benjamin's silly note, after she'd blown her nose. Papa and his partner, a Boyd great-uncle, had operated a haberdasher's shop in Saint Louis, selling gloves and hats and canes and things like that for elegant gentlemen. The partner liked the haberdashery business, but Papa had got tired of it after a while. He'd told Mama and his Boyd relatives that he didn't intend to spend the rest of his life in Missouri in his own hometown selling vests and cravats. "No thank you!" So in spite of Mama's earnest opposition, Papa had sold his share of the store to the Boyd great-uncle.

And then he had done an underhanded thing. He had secretly sent part of the money he got from his partner out to his older brother, Owen, in Arizona Territory. Papa didn't tell us about this until he came home one night the last week in May with five train tickets and told us that we were all going out to Leacock, Arizona Territory, in a couple of weeks' time, to look at the land Owen had bought for us. It was a lot of acres in a valley where there was a stream that was a "babbling brook." What was left of the money Papa planned to use to develop the good land for raising beef cattle. That's what Owen was doing on the ranch that adjoined Papa's. It thrilled Papa to think that together he and his brother owned a whole little valley. He even had it in mind to call it Boyd's Valley. By crumbs, Papa thought big!

Mama wasn't so sure. She called the land Boyd's Folly under her breath to Papa's sister, Aunt Willa. Aunt Willa agreed. She knew Papa as well as we did,

and she knew Uncle Owen a whole lot better. Ann
Viola and William and I had never met him. He'd
gone out West before I was born and never once
come back to Saint Louis to visit. It seemed he and
Aunt Willa never got along. But Uncle Owen wrote
letters. In the one we'd received last January he'd
said that he'd recently "taken to himself a beauteous
bride and put an end to his mournful bachelorhood
for all time." He didn't say what his wife's name was.
The rest of the letter had been about his ranch and
how much money he expected to make from it—once
he "really got it going." That was what had whetted
Papa's appetite to sell out to his partner and write
Uncle Owen to buy some land for him too.

Mama had finally given in to Papa and said that
it was a good thing it would soon be June and the
three of us would be out of school. She didn't want
us to take time away from our educations to see the
West. But she stood firm on one thing—she wouldn't
sell our house in Saint Louis. Papa's cousin, Jonah
Boyd, would live in it and keep up the lawn and
flowers while we were away. I could read Mama's
mind some of the time. I knew she was figuring that
once Papa had seen the land in Arizona Territory,
he might be satisfied by just the view.

And, oh, she had worked hard on him all the way
west on the train. Just about all she talked about was
how hard farming was. She knew. She'd been born
and raised on a farm herself. Being a haberdasher for

twenty years didn't put muscles in a man's arms and callouses on his hands. Papa didn't even much fancy working in our vegetable garden. He didn't have any more muscles than an oyster. He'd rather play whist. He was one of the best whist players in the state of Missouri, according to him.

I stole a look at Mama now, wondering what she'd think of Mr. Benjamin's note. She snorted again. "That Benjamin man is completely crazy, Damaris. I wish to heaven that we'd never set eyes on him. And he was such a good hymn singer too. I could pass the hot place where he will be sizzling someday and never offer him a glass of water. Giving this ridiculous note to you is adding insult to injury. I suppose he is getting even with you for talking to him." She handed the paper back to me. "You tear it up. You're younger than I am. It's too hot in here for me to do it."

"Hey, don't tear it up," said William, coming alive all at once. "Let me take a look at it." He grabbed it from me, read it, and laughed. "A elephant? Hey, was Mr. Benjamin with a circus? Why would he give Damaris an elephant?"

"A elephant?" Ann Viola squealed.

"Oh, it's a silly, ugly joke, children," said Mama. "That very fine gentleman, Mr. Benjamin, defrauded your father of five hundred dollars two nights ago, and then he left the train along with all those other men."

"And Papa, too!" William added, frowning.

Mama sighed, fanning herself with her handkerchief. "Yes, along with every other male passenger aboard this train. It's a mercy they didn't jump off, too. It was just like rats deserting the sinking ship, wasn't it?"

That was just how it had been. We'd stopped for a half hour to eat lunch at the café in the depot in Spar City and that's where we got deserted. While I had been chewing on a biscuit that must have been made out of plaster of Paris instead of flour, a man in a red shirt had thrown open the double doors of the café and yelled at the top of his lungs, "It's *gold,* boys! There's been *gold* found a hundred miles from here!"

Every man in the café had jumped to his feet with a wild look on his face. Papa had got up, too, so fast he still had a forkful of mashed potatoes in one hand. He had choked down the meat in his mouth in one big gulp and said deep in his throat, *"Gold?"*

"Gold!" Everybody in the café was calling out the magic word. The waitresses had backed off to the wall out of the way. I guess they knew what to expect, because they were living out on the frontier and had seen buffalo stampedes. In a minute the stampede started. The men headed for the doors and out into the street of Spar City, where the heat at noon was enough to stun an ox. One of the stampeders knocked down the railroad man beside the door. He was hold-

ing his watch in his hand, ready to call out that it was time for us to stop eating and board again to keep on schedule. I had kept my eye on him all the time I was chewing, because when he yelled that lunch was over, we had to rush for the train. I hated that man by now. He'd cut our lunch short in seven different towns already, so it was very satisfying to see a big passenger send him sprawling as he ran past.

Papa wasn't quite so fast on his feet as the other men. He turned around at Mama's cry of "Charlie, come back!" as he ran out in pursuit of the others. But Papa didn't return to our table. We found him five minutes later aboard the train getting his valise and one carpetbag down out of our baggage. He gave each one of us a quick hug and kiss and told Mama in front of everyone, "Lucy, dearest, I'll come see you on our land in Boyd Valley when I've got back that five hundred dollars I lost. Tell Owen and his bride to take good care of all of you for me until then. Trust yourselves to Owen. I'll get a message to you as soon as I can. And don't you worry. I won't ever play cards again." And he was off, hurrying down the aisle.

Our whole car had gone completely crazy. All the men were grabbing baggage, kissing their families, and rushing off the train with people clutching at them, crying and yelling. William would have run off with Papa, but Mama collared him as he started down the aisle too and pushed him back into his seat.

"You are too young for gold fever!" she cried at him.

"No, I'm not!" He tried to struggle up, but she and I held him down. Finally I sat down on him. While he was struggling and I was sitting, I looked out the train window at the platform, filled with men who were streaming off the train's cars. None of them got on board again, though I could hear ladies and children calling out to them from the whole length of the train. Some of the men waved and blew kisses, which proved they hadn't lost their minds completely, but they all disappeared down the platform steps. Off to the goldfields!

Trains have no mercy at all. Our train started chugging west right on schedule while Papa and the other men ran away to wherever the gold had been found a hundred miles from Spar City. We didn't even know what direction it had been found in. Wherever he was bound, it was a long way from Spar City, and each time the wheels clicked on the rails, we were farther away from him.

I got off William and heard Ann Viola wail, "Papa's gone."

Mama wasn't about to comfort her. She had her face buried in her handkerchief. She was murmuring, "My Lord, I read about gold fever in the Saint Louis newspapers, but I didn't believe a word of it. They said it was a disease. And it is. Those men went completely mad!"

"You didn't let me go," William accused her. "I could have helped Pa a lot."

I kept quiet. I figured gold fever was a disease that afflicted men for the most part—like "get-rich-quick." Finding gold was just another form of that ailment. But then Papa was, to his own way of thinking, doing something a bit more than just going out after gold. He knew we needed to mend our fortunes and wanted to get back the five hundred dollars he'd lost.

He'd lost it to Mr. Benjamin, who had called me a terror on two feet because I'd talked to him last night about his winning Papa's money in a poker game in the smoking car of the train.

Papa was a whist player, not a poker player. I had let Mr. Benjamin have it right between the eyes after he told me that he had no intention of returning Papa's money to him.

I said, "Mr. Benjamin, my father thought he was going to play whist with you."

Mr. Benjamin was a thin, little man with a bushy gray beard and eyeglasses and little greenish eyes. He had held the lapels of his frock coat in both hands and stared at me. Then he said, "Little lady, I have never heard of a man who could not be held to account for agreeing to play poker when someone sug-

gested that he play that game instead of whist. Your
father knew what he was doing."

"But you won all his money. You will never walk
the streets of New Jerusalem," I told him.

"I do not intend to walk them, little girl. Do you
know that you are a real terror on two feet?"

"Perhaps you think I am, but I intend to walk the
streets of heaven, Mr. Benjamin. You are treading in
evil paths, even if you are a hymn singer."

He laughed, then said something very mysterious.
"I may have done your father a favor in beating him
at poker, Miss Boyd. Your father is the sort of man
who would draw to an inside straight."

"My father *is* straight," I flared at him. Turning
around, I went back to my seat. Truly I didn't understand Mr. Benjamin at all. And now he'd said he
was giving me an elephant!

And I'd thought that I was going to enjoy the train
ride out West! We were traveling in style, the way
Papa liked to do things. Other passengers had to sit
up in their seats all the way to wherever they were
going, but not us. In Saint Louis we had boarded a
maroon-colored Pullman car that had *Queen of the
Prairies* painted in gold letters on the sides. We sat
up all day, but at night the train porters performed
a magical trick; part of the wall came down and
turned into beds, one on top of the other. They were
called "berths" and worked on hinges.

The *Queen of the Prairies* was a very elegant car by daytime too. It had gold-trimmed mirrors, polished silver trappings, and shiny wood on the car's sides, a ceiling painted with scenery of mountains and lakes and cherubs, and a red Brussels carpet on the floor. The windows had curtains of red damask, and at one end of the car there was an organ. Near the other end was a gleaming, black pot-bellied stove to keep passengers warm in winter.

There were other cars on the train that went from Saint Louis to San Diego, California. As first-class passengers we could go anywhere on the train we wanted to. We walked through the third-class passenger cars that were jam-packed with people on benches and through the second-class cars that were quite a bit nicer. There were blanket-wearing Indians in these cars. The conductor told me that the chiefs had passes to ride free, because the Government had made treaties with them. These were the first Indians I'd ever seen. You couldn't tell what went on in their minds from looking at their faces, but they seemed peaceful enough. Some of them we saw looked downright bored. But I didn't know half as much about Indians then as I do now!

Though we ate lunch in depot cafés, as first-class passengers we had breakfast and supper in the dining car. We got to know that car very well. And once Ann Viola and I walked through the smoking car where all the men seemed to gather, but it was so thick in there with cigar and pipe smoke that we skedaddled out as fast as we could, coughing. Then we stood for what seemed hours on end on the platform at the rear of the last car of the train—the observation car, it was called. Standing there, you got a good view of the country that you were just leaving as well as what you had left a while before.

That satisfied Ann Viola and me—but not William. He didn't want to see what we'd passed but what was coming. He wanted to go up into the cab of the engine with the engineer and man who fed coal and wood into the boilers to power the train. But the conductor had told him that he couldn't do that. No passengers were allowed up in front unless they were owners of the railroad or maybe a president of the United States who wanted to see how the country looked as the train met it head-on. William got the idea that it was a place for "leaders of men," which only made him want to visit it more. He'd felt insulted by having to look backwards instead of frontwards.

The second night out from Saint Louis, William had decided to become friendly with someone he thought might be able to get him up in the engine. The man he picked was Mr. Benjamin, who turned out to be our mortal enemy. Mr. Benjamin sat across the aisle of our car one seat ahead of us. He looked very honest and prosperous in his top hat and black frock coat, so William got the fleabite idea in his brain that Mr. Benjamin might be a railroad owner.

So, stopping in his game of leap frog in the aisles with a boy bound for California, William went right up to Mr. Benjamin and said, loudly enough for me to hear, "Hey, mister, can you fix things so I can go up and stand out on the cowcatcher of the engine? That's the real front part of the train, you know."

I heard Mr. Benjamin laugh. He called out to the whole car, embarrassing our family, "Here's a boy who wants to get ahead—just as far ahead as he can, huh?"

"Yes, sir." William wasn't one bit shy. He took Mr. Benjamin's notice for an invitation and sat down beside him to talk. Later on, after we'd heard a stirring sermon about the heathen Indians from a preacher going out to New Mexico Territory and had sung some hymns while Mama played the organ, Ann Viola and I talked with William about Mr. Benjamin. He wasn't a railroad owner, but he was an important businessman who traveled all over the West.

Mr. Benjamin sort of took up with us after that. He shared our table at breakfast and supper. Though he was very polite to Mama, Ann Viola, and me, he talked mostly to Papa, and he made a positive pet out of William, which was disgusting to see. Papa liked his company, which showed just how much good taste in people Papa has. By coincidence Mr. Benjamin was going to Leacock, Arizona Territory, too. He was also going to buy land. He expected to set up a business in the town. That didn't interest Papa very much. He was too full up with the idea of the ranch.

The fourth night out from Saint Louis Papa went off with Mr. Benjamin to the smoking car.

And that's where Papa went from whist to poker and lost almost all of our money to Mr. Benjamin. "Card shark" was what Mama called Mr. Benjamin. She knew that gamblers traveled riverboats on the Mississippi River, so she guessed that they rode trains, too, cheating people. For a time she had it in mind herself to ask Mr. Benjamin to return our money, but Papa had a fit when she told him what she planned to do. I heard him say, "No, Lucy, you'd shame me!"

So she kept quiet—but not me! Papa hadn't said those words to me. I marched right up to Mr. Benjamin, bearded him, and said what I said. But I was careful to do it in private where nobody overheard us talking.

Afterwards I told Mama what I'd said to him, though to make her feel better I told her a white lie. "Mr. Benjamin looked a little bit ashamed of what he did to Papa," I said. The truth of the matter was that he hadn't acted one bit shamed.

"Shamed enough to give the money back to you, Damaris?" Mama asked.

"Not that ashamed. We are kerflummoxed."

She said, "That old whelp of a man!"

In our minds, the matter was ended. We would have to borrow money from Uncle Owen to get us back home. But now everything looked hopeless. Papa had left the train and so had Mr. Benjamin, and when Mr. Benjamin left, so had my hopes of getting onto him about the money again. Until then, I hadn't truly given up on him. I was giving him sad and melancholy glances and preparing the right words to say the next time I got him alone. He had been right about one thing. I had it in mind to be a "terror on two feet" as far as he was concerned until we got off at Leacock. They didn't nickname me "Don't Give Up the Ship Boyd" at my school in Saint Louis for nothing.

And then, by crumbs, gold fever struck my plans to dust and ruined everything.

And on top of that, Mr. Benjamin had rubbed it in by writing me such a nasty note!

We went to supper that night in the dining car, because supper was paid for already on our tickets. So was breakfast the next morning. At noon we should be in Leacock. Mama had two ten-dollar gold pieces in her purse, and I had a five-dollar gold piece Aunt Willa Boyd had given me on my thirteenth birthday. That was all of our worldly wealth, and it wasn't much.

None of us was hungry that night. I didn't want

my terrapin soup or oysters or antelope steak. I wanted Papa back with us, even though I hadn't spoken to him for over twenty-four hours because I was so angry at him for playing poker.

We'd had the same dining-car waiter all along. He liked us and talked a lot. We knew that he must have seen Papa and the other men leave the train, and that night he was extra pleasant to Mama. He pitied lost ladies and forlorn families, I suspected. As he brought the strawberry sherbet, he told her, "Don't you fret, ma'am. Your husband'll be back before you know it."

"Maybe Papa will," I told him, finding out that I had some appetite for the sherbet after all, "but I surely hope that horrible Mr. Benjamin stays out in the goldfields forever."

"Oh?" The waiter looked very surprised. "He's a fine gent. He rides our trains a lot."

"Then you better not play poker with him," Ann Viola piped up. I'd told her what had happened.

William explained, "Papa did and lost all of our money."

"William!" Mama scolded, as the waiter poured her coffee out of a heavy silver pot.

To make Papa look better in the waiter's estimation, I added, "Yes, Mr. Benjamin said that Papa was the sort of man who would draw to an inside straight!"

"Tsk!" Holding the coffeepot, the waiter shifted his gaze toward the ceiling. "That is very bad."

"What does it mean?" I asked him, before Mama could stop me.

"It means that. . . ." He hesitated, then looked at Mama. "It's easier to show you than to tell you. Do you want me to, after I've cleared off the table?"

Mama hesitated until I hissed at her, "We ought to know so we can tell Papa what he did wrong."

When everything had been taken off the table, our waiter and another waiter got out some cards from somewhere and demonstrated for us how people played the game of poker. It surely wasn't anything we'd learned in school, though William tried to pretend that he knew all about it. Under the lamp that swayed over the table, as we rattled across more miles of rocks and sagebrush in the night, they showed how a couple of kinds of poker were played. I thought the game looked quite simple, but they said it had a lot of "fine points" to it that weren't to be learned overnight.

Papa, they told us, had probably played draw poker and when the waiters showed us what a straight was, I guessed that Papa should have stuck to whist. He must have expected an angel perching on his shoulder when he bet. I guessed he'd never given himself much of a chance to win. If he'd drawn to an inside straight, it would have meant that he'd hoped to draw only one special card—such as a ten in the middle of a queen, jack, nine, and eight series instead of hoping for a king or an eight at the end of the

queen, jack, ten, and nine series. A king or an eight
would give him a double chance to win. Papa had
surely taken an awful chance—and lost because of it.

I sighed. Maybe Mr. Benjamin hadn't been so
wicked after all. According to the waiters, he was a
very respectable man. I decided to change their good
opinions of him. So I took that infernal note out of
my pocket and gave it to one of them saying, "Mr.
Benjamin's a crazy man. This ought to prove it to
you. You don't know him at all. He ought to be
locked up."

The waiter unfolded the note and read it. He
didn't say a word, only whistled. Then he passed the
note to the other man, who gave me a startled look
over the rim of his spectacles before he returned it
to me. He said, "Well, missy, it looks to me like you
own Mr. Benjamin's elephant. He must have been
mighty partial to you."

I exploded all the way to the ceiling, which in this
car was painted to resemble Niagara Falls. "Partial
to me? He hates me!"

All at once Mama put her hand on top of mine.
Hers was trembling. "Hush, Damaris." Then she
asked our waiter, "Do you mean to tell me that there
truly is an elephant?"

"Oh, yes, at least that's what Mr. Benjamin has
been calling it for the last couple of years. I guess he's
getting tired of it. Its real name is Nomad, like he
says."

While the rest of us sat around with our mouths open, William rushed in. "Where is it?"

"It's aboard."

"Aboard this train?" squeaked Ann Viola.

"Right this very moment?" I wanted to know.

"Sure it is." Our waiter laughed. "Wherever Mr. Benjamin goes, it goes. It does all of its traveling by train."

2

LEACOCK

My Lord! An elephant? An elephant aboard this train? Mr. Benjamin had to be a circus man then. I'd seen elephants, gray ones in circuses that came to Saint Louis. What was more, I'd read a book about Siam once. Because of it I knew that white elephants were very rare and very valuable. There were express cars attached to our train. Maybe the elephant was in one of them?

"What express car is my elephant in?" I asked the waiter.

"Express car?" He looked puzzled, then he said, "No express car, little lady. It's on a special flatcar. Mr. Benjamin always loads it on a flatcar once he's got it apart."

"Apart?" Mama was looking very puzzled.

"Sure, he wouldn't put a knocked-down building in an express car when it could travel easier and cheaper on a flatcar."

"A building?" William got the words out before I could. He sounded disgusted. An elephant would have been very interesting.

"What kind of building?" Mama wanted to know.

"It's a hotel, ma'am. A traveling hotel. Boards painted white and some canvas and furniture, all packed up and on the move. That's why it's called the Nomad. It's been put up and taken down all over the West."

"Good heavens. A traveling hotel." Mama turned to me. "What in the world are we supposed to do with a collapsed hotel?"

I was still speechless and could only shake my head at Mama. Our waiter told her, "Whatever your daughter makes up her mind to do. The hotel's hers, and it gets off at Leacock when you do. That's as far as the flatcar goes."

"I shall fill an early grave if this madness goes on much longer," Mama protested. "Damaris isn't twenty-one. She's a minor."

"So's Papa—out after gold," grumbled William. I caught the sour-grapes tone in his voice. He was jealous of me because I'd been given a hotel.

I read the note Mr. Benjamin had sent me once more while Mama said to the waiter, "I wish to heaven that we had my husband here right this moment. We need his advice badly."

"You know," the second waiter told me, "I wish Mr. Benjamin had gifted me with the old Nomad.

Leacock's booming now that the railroad's come through. That old hotel could make a mint in a hurry. It could make you rich quicker than you'd believe."

Finally I was taking it all in! I owned a hotel. By crumbs, it was mine! But all the same I didn't like this get-rich-quick idea he was talking about.

Mama said what I was thinking. "Heaven forbid, not more get-rich-quick! Mr. Benjamin may have turned at the last moment from the ways of a hyena, but what are we to do with a hotel?"

"It isn't yours, Mama," came from Ann Viola, who sometimes thought quite clearly for one so young. "Damaris, what are you going to do with it?"

"I'll tell you," Mama said sharply to her. "We are going to sell it just as soon as we can. It ought to fetch a nice sum somewhere." She asked our waiter, "Will you please inform the men on this train that we now own Mr. Benjamin's hotel and are willing to sell it to the highest bidder."

The other waiter grinned at her. "What men, ma'am? There's nobody aboard except for old grandpas and boys your son's age, remember?"

"That's so, Mama," said Ann Viola.

William was being thoughtful. He asked himself more than anyone else, "I wonder why Mr. Benjamin called it a 'white elephant'? It sounds like a funny thing to say."

Our waiter nodded. "Well, sonny, you know what

a white elephant can be—something troublesome that somebody doesn't really want anymore. Maybe that's how he felt about lugging that hotel all over the West. He said once he was wearying."

My brother said slowly, "I'll bet that's why he lit out for the goldfields, too." He looked at me and showed me he already thought with the mind of menfolks when he said, "Damaris, maybe he didn't do you so much of a favor after all. Maybe you shouldn't look a gift elephant in the mouth."

Nobody laughed except for the waiters—not even when I said, "No, you might get a tusk in your ear."

Ann Viola said wistfully, "I wish it could have been a real elephant so we could take rides on it."

"Well, it isn't alive, children, and I am very grateful for that," Mama told us sternly. "Give up this silly nonsense and come back to our car, so I can think about this whole mad business some more."

I could hear Mama tossing around in the berth below me while I lay in the upper one staring at the gaslit scenery on the ceiling. Up that high I could reach out and touch one of the fat cherubs just over my head. I knew enough not to argue with Mama over selling my odd present. The whole day had kerflummoxed me plenty.

We arrived in Leacock just in time to find Leacock leaving—or at least people were heading out from it. As we got down out of the *Queen of the Prairies* into a sun so hot that Mama made Ann Viola and me put up our parasols at once, Mama exclaimed, "What on earth is going on here?"

We could see one long, straight, unpaved street with wooden houses and stores on each side. But the street itself was jammed with men in wagons and on horseback. They were all heading north and east in what looked like a parade of people and animals. We were standing on the depot platform at the south end of Leacock with some other lady passengers watching the north-south road that was Leacock's only street.

One of the other ladies, a girl about twenty, I guessed, suddenly let out a terrible shrill yell, "Harry. Harry, I got here. Where are you going, Harry?"

A young man on a bay horse and leading a loaded-down pack mule stopped at the end of the street to look back over his shoulder. Then he turned his horse around and, pulling the mule behind him, came trotting back against the stream of people going away.

"Sweetheart! Alice!" he called. He rode right up to the platform, swept the girl off her feet, kissed her in front of everybody, and put her down again. Then just as if we weren't all listening, he asked, "Alice, will you marry me?"

I stared at Alice, wondering what she would say. Nobody had ever asked me that question, and I was curious. I'd seen Alice before. She had red cheeks most of the time, but now her whole face was sort of white. "Harry?" she said very softly.

He leaned down and spoke quickly, "What is it, Alice, yes or no? I haven't got a lot of time just now."

"I don't know, Harry."

"Well, make up your mind, sweetheart." He pointed to a house not far from the depot. "If you decide yes, and want to marry me, that's my mother's house over there, the one with the shingles on the roof. She'll look after you until I come back."

"Harry, where are you going?" Alice demanded.

"The goldfields. There's been a big strike northeast of here."

Alice started to cry. Even over her sobs, I could hear Mama's sniff of fury. Alice didn't pay any attention to anyone but Harry. "I came all the way out here from Topeka because you wrote and asked me to." She stamped her foot. "But, Harry Tucker, I bought a round-trip ticket just in case. I can go home on the eastbound train."

He shook his head at her. My, but he was a handsome young man, with a fine, big, brown mustache. His horse was nice too. "Well, then, Alice, I'll be sorry if you leave, but it ain't every day a man gets a chance to get rich in a hurry." He lifted his hat to all of us, reined the horse away, and went trotting back down the street on his way out of town.

Mama spoke darkly to Alice whoever-her-name was. "It must be the same gold discovery we heard about yesterday. I wonder how they got the news here so quickly."

William was tugging at Mama's sleeve. "That's how." With his other hand he was pointing at the telegraph office on the depot platform, and then he pointed to the pole not far away. I remembered that I'd seen telegraph poles all alongside the railroad tracks. News traveled very swiftly by telegraph. Somebody had sent a telegram from the town where we'd lost Papa. That was why Leacock was clearing out, too. Gold fever was the cause! A dreadful disease!

"Mama," I asked, "Should we send a telegram to Cousin Jonah or Aunt Willa or some of the other Boyds back home?"

She gave me a look that was hotter than the June sunshine. "What would I tell them? What can they do to help us back in Missouri? No, the business I have with the Boyd family has to be with Owen. He's the one who's out here in this godforsaken place."

I had had a good look at the scenery while we pulled into Leacock. It certainly wasn't anything I figured would get painted on the ceiling of a railroad car. It was all tan-colored rocks with here and there— but not often enough—some green bushes. Later on I learned they were creosote bushes. There were sharp, jagged purple mountains to the north and west under a gray-bright sky that looked to me as if it might leak hot quicksilver on us any minute.

The houses in Leacock seemed to be a hundred

years old, they were so bleached by the desert sunshine. I guessed the winds must blow through them
like water through a sieve. It was blowing now, sending grit into our faces. Little whirls of soil and sand
were turning and twisting beside the platform. "Dust
devils" is what they are called—though I hadn't
learned that yet.

No, I didn't care at all for my introduction to
Arizona Territory. Judging from the looks on the
faces of the other women and children on the platform who'd got off the train, they agreed with me.

Just then a man in a dark blue cap and coat came
out of the depot with a paper in his hand and an
important look on his face. He called out, "Is somebody here named Damaris Boyd?"

"That's me, mister." I caught at Mama's hand. Was
it the telegrapher with a message from Papa?

But it was only the Leacock station agent. "There's
a flatcar on this train that I hear has something to
do with you, miss," he told me. He stared down at
me as if he couldn't believe his eyes.

"Yes, sir, it's my hotel."

He was staring over my head at Mama, who was
nodding. He believed her. He said to her, "Well,
we're sidetracking the flatcar here, ma'am. You people will have forty-eight hours to get your shipment
off the car before the eastbound train comes along
to pick up the flatcar."

"Forty-eight hours?" Mama asked him.

"That's what I said, ma'am. A person only hires the use of a flatcar, you know. It belongs to the railroad." He sounded put out at our stupidity.

Mama told him slowly, "I hadn't thought of that."

He sounded satisfied as he told her, "Now you know."

Before Mama could say anything more, the girl named Alice interrupted. She snapped at him, "Bosh to you, sir, and every other man in this part of the world!" Then she picked up the two carpetbags nearest her. While I thought about the forty-eight hours, Alice turned around and got back onto the train she had just left. She wasn't waiting for her Harry. She seemed to be going on to San Diego rather than stay in Leacock even for the eastbound train to arrive. I admired her spunk!

After the station agent had left us, I asked Mama, "What are we going to do about my hotel?"

She was looking after Alice. I read her mind again. She wished we were free to go out to the Pacific Ocean, too. After all, San Diego was a lot closer than Massachusetts and the Ness family.

Finally she gathered herself together and told me, "I think we'd better find out first of all how far away your Uncle Owen lives from this town. Perhaps he'll have some ideas." She touched William on the shoulder. "William, go into the depot and see if you can't find some nice gentleman to come out here and give us some information about this part of the country."

From what I'd seen of Leacock, I doubted if William would be able to find a gentleman anywhere. What's more I wasn't sure that he'd know one if he did find one. After all, he'd thought Mr. Benjamin was a railroad owner and a very nice man.

My first glimpse of what William brought back with him made me wonder even more. It was a man all right. All the hair on his face proved that it was. He had long gray and brown locks, bushy eyebrows, and a small pug nose sticking out of a tangle of whiskers curling up at the ends. His mouth couldn't be seen at all. What I could see of his eyes under those eyebrows wasn't much, but his cheeks were tanned brown. When he took off his plug hat to bow to Mama, I noticed that the bald top of his head was sunburned, too. His black-and-white checkered pants and vest and his black coat looked to me as if they'd been ironed with a waffle iron ten years ago.

"Malachi Ponder, at your service, ma'am," he told Mama. He smiled at her. His teeth were a gold mine all by themselves. No wonder he was still in Leacock. He had his gold fortune. Before Mama could ask him about Uncle Owen, he asked her, "Are you by chance a widow woman?"

That made even William gasp; the man sounded almost as though he hoped that Mama was. She said, "No, my husband's gone to the goldfields. He will be along quite soon, I suspect." That should have stopped Mr. Ponder in his tracks.

He did seem disappointed and stared hard at me, then looked even more disappointed. I figured he figured that it was too bad I was so young.

"There aren't many eligible ladies in these parts," he told Mama. By now the other passengers had left the platform, either heading into Leacock or getting back onto the train. One old man was left sitting on the platform as if he was waiting for someone to come and get him. I thought that he looked mad as a moulting rooster caught in a rainstorm, more than likely because he was too feeble to head for the goldfields. This made me wonder even more about Mr. Ponder being here. He looked able-bodied enough, though he wasn't anything we'd have in our parlor Saturday night.

But his manners were good enough. "No offense, ma'am. It's just that what this country needs is a whole boatload of unwed females of the fitting age." He glanced at me again, making me want to tell him, "I am thirteen and reputed to be a terror on two feet."

Mama thought he was amusing. Either that or she was going to become hysterical. We all laughed at him. The idea of a boatload of ladies in the desert *was* laughable.

He laughed too. "What can I do for you folks?"

Mama recovered herself and told him, "Mr. Ponder, it seems difficult to believe, but we have brought a hotel along with us. I assure you it's true. I am not suffering from sunstroke."

Ponder nodded. "Your boy already told me that. It's the Nomad. He says you've got it on a flatcar."

And just as he said it, we got our first view of my hotel. Our train pulled out of the station, heading for California and making so much noise that Ponder didn't even try to talk over it. When the train had passed, he pointed to where its last cars had been. There, on a siding beside the regular tracks, stood one very lonely-looking flatcar. There wasn't much to see except for a long shape covered over with gray-white canvas tarpaulin and at one end a heap of things under more canvas and lashed on with ropes. Because the things were lots of different sizes, I guessed they must be my furniture. By crumbs, I did own a hotel! I wondered how well equipped the Nomad was with things a hotel would have to have.

Mama sighed. "Mr. Ponder, did you know Mr. Benjamin?"

"Yes, ma'am. Some years ago back in West Texas. I hear he donated the Nomad to you folks?" He didn't seem to me to be very surprised.

"Mr. Ponder," said Mama, "you heard correctly. We have only forty-eight hours to get the thing off the flatcar. Do you suppose that you could do that, and then try to sell it for us here in Leacock? We'll pay you out of the money we get for it."

He bowed again. "For a lady in distress, I will do that, of course. Where will you be staying in the meantime?"

"We are related to a Mr. Owen Boyd, who has a ranch not far from here," Mama replied. "We're going to stay with him. Do you know where it is?"

"With Owen, huh?" I thought Ponder sounded surprised now.

"Yes, he's my husband's brother."

"He's married," said Ann Viola all at once.

Ponder looked from my sister to the blazing sky. "Yep, Owen's got himself a purty little wife all right. I hear tell she was a pretty expensive item to deal with."

I thought that was an odd way of saying that somebody's wife was extravagant, but then people way out West spoke differently, I supposed.

"How far away is Owen's place from here?" Mama wanted to know.

"Thirty miles maybe. He lives closer to Switzer Wells than Leacock."

"How can we get there right away, Mr. Ponder?"

"I'll take you folks in my wagon. I've got a dandy one."

"What about the hotel?" I jerked my head toward the flatcar.

"Never fear, little girl. I'll get my helper to unload it, and he'll guard it while we're away."

Mama told him, "Mr. Ponder, I have to be honest

with you. We have very little money right now, but I want to pay for the use of the wagon."

"It don't matter, ma'am. Arthur and I won't mind waiting as long as need be." He eyed the flatcar. "Well, let's get going so we can get back here before Arthur's got to make a decision on where to put the Nomad after he's unloaded it. Are these here your satchels and carpetbags?"

I began to wonder about Mr. Ponder. He ought to be able to guess that the baggage was ours. After all, everybody else had left the platform. Later on I was to learn that this was Mr. Ponder's way of doing things. Though I didn't know it at the time and neither did anybody else, except maybe him, Mr. Ponder was going to become very important in our lives. Mama and I followed him down the depot steps with William at our heels, carrying two satchels, and Ann Viola, with her doll, bringing up the rear. I asked Mama, "What do you suppose Mr. Ponder meant by saying that we'd be back here? Do you expect to come back?"

"No, I hadn't expected to except to board an eastbound train. I don't know what he meant." She gave me a glance out of the corner of one eye. "It was a queer thing to say, wasn't it? He sounded almost as if he was trying to tell us something about Owen, didn't he?"

By crumbs, she was right. Mr. Ponder didn't seem

to think we'd stay long with Owen and his new bride.

Down on the ground, while dust devils swirled around our skirts, Mama handed me her parasol to hold while she took off the linen duster she'd worn all the way from Saint Louis to protect her dress. She tucked it under her arm saying, "This is a hellish climate, Damaris. The Pacific Ocean sounds nicer all the time. It's too hot to wear this. If it weren't for Owen Boyd being here, and if we had a lot of money, that's where we would have gone, too. To San Diego. We'd have let your father worry about us and hunt for us—instead of our waiting around for him." She bit her lip. "As long as we are here, I shall lower my standards somewhat, though I'd rather not show up in front of Owen and his bride covered with dust. You know how elegant some of the Boyds are inclined to be. That remark about his wife's being expensive worries me."

What she said about the Boyds being elegant was true. According to Aunt Willa, Uncle Owen was a real dandy. And there were no flies on cousin Jonah either when it came to looking spruce. Their foreheads might bulge a bit, but the hats on top of them were right up-to-the-minute in style.

As we traipsed after Mr. Ponder, who seemed headed for a building with the words "Livery Stable" over it, I wondered about a batch of things. How was Papa doing in the goldfields? Where were the goldfields exactly? What would Uncle Owen and his ranch be like? And what about his extravagant wife? Was she a snob?

Just then William pushed past me, yelling, "Hey, Mr. Ponder, where do I go from here?" William was running—running in this awful heat. Not me. I kept my head under my parasol and walked like a lady, the way Mama did.

3

BOYD VALLEY

On the way to Uncle Owen's ranch I learned something about Mr. Ponder. Keeping quiet wasn't his strong point. When he wasn't talking, he was asking questions of William and me as we sat beside him on the front seat of his three-seater platform wagon. It was a handsome vehicle all right, plum-colored with Brewster-green trim on the wheels and a green canopy top with fringe all around it. And it had good springs. If it hadn't, we'd all have been tossed out onto the road, which seemed to me to be made out of pebbles and bigger rocks.

As we started out Mr. Ponder told us first of all about his team of horses, Victor and Treasureen. They weren't exactly matched. Victor was a dapple gray and Treasureen a sorrel, but they were good horses.

When I asked about the sorrel's queer name, Ponder told me that it was an Irish word for "little treasure." By crumbs, the horse wasn't one bit little, but all the same her name let me know that there was some Irish blood in Mr. Ponder. And so there was. His mother had come from County Mayo to Philadelphia and there married an American. Mr. Ponder had been born in Pennsylvania. After that, he talked on and on while Mama and Ann Viola sat shaded, but sweltering, under the top behind William and him and me.

Ponder had come out West right after the Civil War and had been out here ever since. He'd done all sorts of work—blacksmithing, carpentering, and horse doctoring—and he'd tried both gold and silver mining. Now he was a partner in the Leacock livery stable business. This wagon and some other vehicles belonged to him, it seemed.

He had no intention of going off to the goldfields. He claimed he wasn't gifted with miner's luck. "So I quit while I was ahead of the game and went into business," he told me.

Because we were on the subject of business, I told him how I had got my hotel.

"That'll be quite a surprise to your pa when he finds out, won't it?" he said to me. Then he added, "Maybe he'll hit it lucky in the diggings."

"Well, maybe so." I wondered about some other things while we went on our way to Boyd Valley, which is what I called it in my head. Who was this Arthur, who was supposed to get my hotel off the flatcar? We'd never set eyes on him at the livery stable, but we'd heard Ponder tell a small boy who was oiling some harness pieces to "go find Arthur and tell him to unload the flatcar at the depot and guard with his life what he takes off it."

And why was Mr. Ponder so interested in whether Mama was married or not? I figured from what he'd asked her and the other things he said that he was single. I was too polite to ask him if this was fact, so instead I said as we drove past some strange-looking plants, "What are those, please? Out there, I mean? The ones that seem to be trees."

"They *are* trees. That's ironwood and mesquite, and those spiny things are cactus plants. There's lots of different plants here even if it is the desert. If it wasn't the time of day it is, you'd be able to see that the desert has lots of animals, too. Most of 'em have the good sense not to come out in the daytime." He laughed in his beard. "They aren't like human folks. If you had more time, we'd have waited to travel after dark when it's cooler. Oh well, it ain't all that hot today, and we've got plenty of water along with us."

That last remark made me sigh and wipe the perspiration off my forehead with the back of my hand. "Not all that hot!" It was broiling even under the canopy. It wasn't that it was Saint Louis wet hot. That kind of heat made you melt in your clothes. This was like the air coming right out of the oven door when there's a cake baking. That heat and the white-gray dust blowing on me made me want to scratch where I was itching. I didn't do it, though. But because William was a boy and could get away with it better, he scratched. Then my brother asked Mr. Ponder straight out, "Have you got any kids? Is Arthur your kid?"

"No, Maude and I were never blessed."

Ann Viola asked from behind me, "Who was Maude?" She didn't know what "blessed" meant the way he had said it.

Before she could ask why he and Maude never went to church and embarrass all of us, I told her, "Mr. Ponder means that he and his wife never had any children."

"Who was Maude?" Ann Viola asked again.

"My wife. The light of my life until she died two years ago."

"Oh," came from William. Then he asked an awful question, "How did that happen?"

"William!" said Mama.

Ponder comforted her. "I don't take offense, ma'am. Maude never took to this part of the country. She was a delicate creature. She never took to Kansas or Texas or California either—or even to Oregon or Washington Territory. She always wanted to go back home." He let out a sigh.

Mama asked softly, "Where was her home?"

"Boston, Massachusetts, ma'am."

As Mama let out a long, deep sigh, too, he went on, "One morning Maude didn't get up. She said she'd decided to take to her bed and expire. And six months later that's just what she did. I offered to take her back home for a visit, but she claimed it was too late. She said she didn't have the strength for the trip. That was before the train came out here, so we would have had to travel by stagecoach." He added, "The train came too late for my dear old girl."

I said, "I think maybe it went off to California too soon for us." I was getting cross. I wasn't really one bit interested in Uncle Owen. As a matter of fact, I was peeved with him. If he hadn't written Papa such luring letters about his ranch and the land, we wouldn't be in this terrible mess. Each hot and horrible mile we traveled heading toward two solid rock buttes made me suspect that Alice whatever her name was had done the smart thing in going on to the Pacific Ocean and San Diego.

By crumbs, I surely hoped that Uncle Owen would have a nice house with soft beds and a bathtub! I turned around to look at Mama. She was paler than usual. I hoped that our new aunt would be an understanding lady and not ask Mama a lot of wearying questions about the trip. Mama wasn't the strongest person in the world. I knew that. The doctor had told Aunt Willa and Papa so right after Ann Viola had been born. Papa and William should have come out here alone—just the two of them. If there'd been only William, Papa wouldn't have dared desert the train for the diggings. But if he had, he could have taken William with him. There was nothing William liked better than dirt.

As it was, Papa had put a burden on Mama—not to mention on me. I tried a smile on Mama. That should show her that I still had some sand and spirit. If she needed to, she could lean on me.

"Don't give up the ship," I told her. "It'll be nice at Uncle Owen's and you can rest up."

"It's pleasant there," agreed Mr. Ponder. "Owen Boyd's got plenty of water. It ain't all boulders where he is. There's good grass."

"We know," said my brother. "That's why he plans to raise cattle. There has to be grass for them."

Mr. Ponder's voice, when he answered, sounded careful. "Far as I know, Owen hasn't got around to raisin' much beef yet. He had some horses for a time, but he hasn't got them anymore neither, and I hear his mules are goin', too."

"Oh," said William, who doted on horses and yearned for one.

Ponder explained, "That's because of Owen's wife, of course."

"Of course," I heard Mama saying, just to show that she had half heard Mr. Ponder. He'd been very nice to us, complete strangers. Maybe, though, he ex-

pected to make a good profit on my hotel when he
sold it. I asked him all at once, "Is Uncle Owen the
kind of man who'd draw to an inside straight in a
poker game? I've never met him."

He jerked on the team's reins so hard they stopped
dead in a cloud of dust that floated back, making me
cough. He turned one hazy blue eye on me. I'd
shocked him good and proper. "By the powders of
war, where did you learn about things like that, little
lady?"

I told him about Papa's lack of ability at poker and
what little I knew about the game he'd played with
Mr. Benjamin. Then I asked, "What about our Uncle
Owen? Is he?" I hoped he wasn't.

First Ponder nodded, then slowly he shook his head
while he made clucking noises that started the team
up again. "He's in good hands now that he's got married. His relations will be working for him, his wife's
folks, I mean. They won't expect to be paid."

"Golly, he sounds stingy," put in William.

Mama was listening in too. "Owen's bride must
have a lot of relatives."

"She does." I saw Mr. Ponder glance over his
shoulder at Mother. He said, "Things aren't exactly
like Saint Louis out here, ma'am."

"Heavens above, you don't need to tell me that,
Mr. Ponder. But I did know Owen. I'm looking for-
ward to finding his ranch an outpost of civilization

in this wilderness. His wife must be a very gracious
person to have all of her family around her. Owen
really must like them a great deal."

Mr. Ponder didn't speak. He grunted, then cleared
his throat as he swung his team around to avoid a
boulder in the middle of the road. It seemed to me
that he was through chatting. So I sat on the wagon
seat thinking and asking myself about Uncle Owen.
I wondered if William was wondering, too. It didn't
seem to me that he was, for just at that moment he
started whistling the tune he'd sung at a Boyd family
oyster sociable last Christmas. It was "I'm the Boy
That's Bound to Blaze."

We came to Boyd Valley through a gap between
the two buttes. Mr. Ponder reined in the team on
some high ground so everyone could get a look at
the valley. It was hard to believe that a place like it
could exist where it was, but there it was. It was a
long, not very wide valley with a stream running
down the middle. Mr. Ponder had already told us a
mile or so back that the stream fed into the Colorado
River farther west. It was because of the stream that
the valley had grass. Besides the grass and water, it
had some trees and big gray rocks sticking up here
and there. But that was all it had—absolutely all!

"Where's the house?" Ann Viola asked.

Mr. Ponder pointed. "Over there near the trees.
See, there's five of 'em. Yep, Owen's wife's relations
are still here. I thought they would be."

I shaded my eyes with my hand, though it was getting on to sunset, and looked where he was pointing. I could see five small things set in a circle. They didn't look like tents to me, though they had canvas on them. They weren't shaped like tents, and they had poles sticking up out of the tops. There were fires smoking in front of three of them.

Mama asked Mr. Ponder, "What on earth are those?"

"Wickiups, ma'am. Maybe you call them tepees, though they ain't."

"Indians! Owen is living with *Indians!*" She was gasping.

Suddenly Mr. Ponder bent over and took the rifle out from under the seat, jerking my heels off its butt. He held it in one hand and fired it into the air, then yelled an instant afterwards, *"Salman, salman."* Next he shouted, "Hey, Owen, it's me, Malachi. We're coming in." And he slapped the reins on the backs of the team to make them start down the road into the valley.

"What did you just say?" William asked Ponder. "What does *salman* mean?"

"Friend. See there, Owen's coming now. The man on horseback."

Yes, there was somebody riding toward us on a black-and-white horse. When he got closer, I saw that he had a full beard and was wearing a red shirt and broad-brimmed black hat.

"Is that Uncle Owen?" I heard Ann Viola ask Mama.

"I think it might be, but I could be wrong," Mama replied in a strange voice. "But if it is, he's changed a good deal."

It was our uncle, though I didn't think he was any more elegant than any man we'd seen rushing out of Leacock. He recognized Mama right off and reached into the wagon to hug her. He grinned at the three of us when she introduced us, then asked the question we knew he'd ask first of all, "Where's my little brother, Charlie?"

Mr. Ponder told him where, not Mama. Owen took off his hat and mopped his brow with his sleeve. Yes, he had the bulging Boyd forehead too. He said to Mama, "This isn't so good, Lucy. I'd counted on Charlie's helping me build a house for you folks and one for me and Natalie. I'm not much of a carpenter. Well, come on down and meet my bride and her folks, but don't expect them to make any fuss over you. It isn't their way—not with Apaches."

All of our mouths fell open as if we were human flytraps.

"*Apaches?*" Ann Viola squealed from behind me.

William asked, sounding fascinated, "Is Aunt Natalie an Apache?"

"No, she isn't, but her family is." He smiled at us.

"My Lord, how can that be?" Mama had found her voice finally.

"She was captured as a little girl by Apaches and raised in their band. They lived then in the mountains of Sonora, down in Old Mexico. She doesn't know who her real parents were."

"Is she a Mexican, Owen?" Mama asked.

He shook his head. "We doubt it. There aren't many blue-eyed Mexicans." He turned his horse around and started off ahead of us, leaving us all with our mouths hanging open.

"Great heavens, Apache in-laws. It surpasses belief. What would Willa have to say about this?" Mama's voice sounded strangled. "What shall we do now?"

"Visit 'em," said Mr. Ponder.

"Will they be dangerous?"

"No, ma'am. I've met Cuchillo—he's Owen's father-in-law—and his band. They've been peaceable for quite a time. They ain't from those White Mountain Apaches that are fighting the U.S. Army all the time. Personally I don't think there's much difference between white folks and Apaches. Apaches are just raised different. You'll always find the good and the bad in both of 'em."

Fifteen minutes later we saw our first Apaches, though it was very clear to me that they weren't seeing us. Each one of them turned his face away as we came by in the wagon. There must have been twenty Indians there. I saw pig-tailed women in moccasins, wide red, blue, and orange skirts, and blouses down to their hips. The men wore red cloths tied around their black long hair, shirts that were as long as night-shirts and were slit along the side, and high moccasins. The men were squatting on the ground or on piles of soft pine boughs.

"Why won't they look at us?" I asked Mr. Ponder, while Uncle Owen led the way to the wickiup farthest away.

"It's Apache manners. Owen can't even speak to his mother-in-law or look her in the face." Ponder laughed. "That's not such a dumb custom either. I had plenty of trouble with Maude's mother, let me tell you. The Apaches have a pretty smart way of get-ting married, too, if you ask me."

Before he could explain Uncle Owen called out, "Natalie," and a woman came out of the tepee. She was tall, slim, and dressed like the Apache women, but her hair was auburn red, not black like theirs.

"She's pretty," breathed William, surprising me. I didn't think he'd notice such a thing.

"You bet she is," agreed Ponder. "She's smart too— educated at a church school in Yuma. She cost Owen four good horses, I hear tell. That makes her an ex-pensive proposition."

"Owen *bought* her?" Mama yelped.

"That's the only way there is to get a wife from the Apaches. He tied the horses out in front of Cuchillo's wickiup, and if she wouldn't water them that would mean she didn't want any part of Owen Boyd for a husband. I hear she made him sweat plenty by not watering his horses for two whole days. She's a proud one, she is!"

"Dear heaven!" Mama was sounding quite weak by now. "What a horrible way of doing things!"

"Well, I ain't so sure of that, ma'am. The bride's family gets something worthwhile instead of paying out plenty for a big wedding to get rid of a daughter and having nothing afterwards but debts and memories."

William liked that idea, of course. He was still laughing when Natalie and Owen came up to the wagon. Yes, Natalie did have blue eyes. She held out her hand to us after Owen had lifted Mama, Ann Viola, and me down out of the wagon. "I am pleased to make your acquaintance," she told Mama.

Mama did the right thing. She kissed her new sister-in-law on the cheek, then murmured, "I hope you will be very happy together."

"Where is Charles?" Natalie asked. Owen told her about the gold strike as we all walked toward their wickiup, except for Mr. Ponder, who was leading the horses to the stream to drink. Natalie started to speak to Owen in what must have been Apache, but all at once she smiled at me and switched to English. "Owen, you will not be going to the goldfields." I couldn't tell by her tone if she was asking a question or giving an order.

Whatever it was, he understood her. "Yes, dear," he said.

The wickiup had blankets inside, a couple of saddles, and that was all except for a leather chest. Mama sat on it while Natalie served us sugared coffee in tin mugs so hot we could scarcely hold them in our hands.

Then Mama asked, "How many cattle do you have, Owen?"

"Only three cows as yet. I'd hoped to get some cash from Charlie, so I could buy some more stock." He looked at Mama. "Can you let me have a hundred dollars, Lucy?"

"We haven't got that much, Owen." I saw Mama slumping down lower on the chest. She'd hoped to borrow from him.

"You don't have a hundred dollars?" He sounded amazed.

"You have your brother Charles to thank for that, Owen." Mama spoke sharply, but she looked sick to me.

"I'll tell him about it, Mama." So while all of us and Mr. Ponder, who'd crowded inside too, drank more coffee I told about Mr. Benjamin and the poker game and about being given my hotel.

Uncle Owen didn't say anything. He only shook his head and listened to what Natalie said to him in Apache. I wished I could understand what that was. It sounded powerful.

We had a supper of corn, beans, nuts, bread baked on the fire outside on a piece of tin, and a strange-tasting meat stew. Mama asked Uncle Owen while we were all eating, "What do you suggest we do now?"

Natalie, whose name we'd found out by now was really Nahtle-tla in Apache, spoke up before he could reply, "How do you like the stew, Mrs. Boyd?"

"Fine, Mrs. Boyd." Mama was still able to smile politely.

"I can tell you how to make it. It's made of hominy, onions, chili peppers, and dried mule meat." Natalie was smiling, too.

"Mule?" said Ann Viola with a spoon to her mouth. We had all used spoons, not forks, throughout supper because there were no forks.

Mama put her plate down on the ground beside the chest. Uncle Owen didn't seem to notice what our opinion of mule was. "Lucy," he told Mama, "I don't think you'd find it very pleasant living here until Charlie comes. If you stay, you'd have to live in a wickiup like the rest of us."

She told him, "To tell the truth, Owen, I had hoped Charlie wouldn't set his heart on living out here at all. We didn't sell our house in Saint Louis. Jonah is living in it now."

"So—Jonah did grow up then?" I knew that cousin Jonah had been considered puny as a child and hadn't been expected to see his tenth birthday. But he was nineteen now. Owen went on, "I think you'd better go back to Leacock and wait for Charlie to show up. It'd be more comfortable there for you."

Mr. Ponder spoke as he ate his last bite of mule,

which he seemed to enjoy as much as if it was beef. "Owen, it'd be nicer for her in Switzer Wells. They can camp at the Casa del Rey. I'm going to try to sell the little lady's hotel for her in Leacock before they go back home. That'll give 'em cash enough for train tickets if they decide to go back to Missouri. Mr. Boyd only bought one-way tickets."

I didn't want to stay in Boyd Valley or Leacock or Switzer Wells, but something had to be done. I could see the tiny twitching motions Mama's feet were making. It was my clue to say something to get us out of the wickiup. "Mama, Mr. Ponder says the best way to travel in the desert is at night. Let's go back to Leacock. When we get things settled or hear from Papa, we'll get in touch with Uncle Owen again."

I saw her look at Mr. Ponder. Oh, he was taking over our lives all right. He was shaking his head. "No, ma'am, I say you'd best go to Switzer Wells. You're just about done in, ain't you?"

"Yes, Mr. Ponder, I am very tired." Mother took one glance at Owen's blankets on the ground and then looked quickly away.

"Then, Mrs. Boyd, with your permission I'll take you to Switzer Wells and the Casa del Rey. Switzer Wells is closest. You and the littlest girl can stay there while your other two go back with me to Leacock."

"Damaris, too?" Mama asked.

"She has to go along. She's got the paper that says she's owner of the hotel. If I can sell it, I suppose she's got to sign some papers to make the sale hold up. Probably you'll have to sign 'em, too. That oughta make things shipshape and legal, Mrs. Boyd."

Mama sighed. She got up and asked, "Owen, may I speak privately with you for a moment?"

They went outside together while Natalie gathered up our tin plates to take them to the stream to wash. Mama and Owen returned soon and she said, "Yes, Mr. Ponder, you may take William and Damaris to Leacock with you. I take it that the railroad hasn't come to Switzer Wells yet?"

"No, ma'am, not yet."

"What about the telegraph?"

Owen said, "There is one all right, Lucy, but it isn't working right now. Mahkto climbed up one of the poles the other day for the green glass on its top. He wanted to make some earrings for Natalie."

"Who's Mahkto?" I asked.

"One of her cousins," said Uncle Owen. He spoke directly to me, "Damaris, while you're in Leacock you can send a message to Willa that you have arrived safely."

"Who's Willa?" asked Mr. Ponder.

"She's my oldest sister, Malachi—Willa Boyd."

"Wed or unwed, Owen?"

"Never wed and never particularly wanted to be as I remember her, Malachi."

By now Natalie had come back. She asked Mr. Ponder, "How is Arthur these days?"

"He's doing just fine."

Mrs. Owen Boyd smiled first at William, then at me. She said quietly, "I hope you will like my cousin Arthur. He has many of the ways of the white people by now." Then she added, "When you see your father, tell him that my husband and I are very happy— even if we live in a wickiup."

"Sure," said William. "We surely will." He liked Owen and Natalie both, I could tell. After all, not everybody in Saint Louis had an Apache for an aunt. I knew him. He wouldn't tell them that she wasn't an Indian. He'd fib and make her a redskinned princess at least.

We left pretty soon afterward for the wagon. When we were out of earshot of everyone but Mr. Ponder, Mama said to me, "Damaris, I never did feel Owen could be counted on in an emergency. Why, he actually expected your father to come to his financial rescue and give him money! And Charlie would have done it. Willa warned me about Owen years ago. Oh, child, I swear if things keep going the way they're going, I'll fill an early grave and it will be here in Arizona Territory!"

"No, you won't, ma'am," said Mr. Ponder. "Everything will turn out all right. Just you watch and see."

4

LITTLE OLD JESS

On the way to Switzer Wells I learned that Mr. Ponder was absolutely right in one thing. The desert wasn't just miles and miles of rocks and nowhere. It had a lot of life in it, but it was night life, as he said. We saw jackrabbits run in front of the wagon, and once he reined in to let a skunk waddle past into some bushes on the other side of the road. An owl sailed over us to land on a cactus just a few minutes before we heard our first coyote howling and then yapping somewhere off in the distance. Those last two things didn't set at all well with us Boyds from Saint Louis.

"Merciful heaven, what was that?" Mama asked Ponder. The sound had made me feel pale around the gills, and William gulped so loud I could hear him.

"Jest a coyote, ma'am."

Ann Viola sounded really scared. "Are there wolves out here, too?"

"Not that I ever seen, but there are plenty of snakes and lizards and buzzards."

Mama sounded acid when she asked, "Is there anything out here that isn't frightening, nasty, and poisonous?"

"It depends on what you think's bad. Sure, there are some sweet-singing birds and mighty tasty quail." The moon was just coming up, so I could see Mr. Ponder's face as he turned to look down at me. "There's a thing called a kiss bug on the desert, too, little lady. A interesting little cuss, the kiss bug."

Oh, I knew what he was driving at all right. "It doesn't interest me one bit, Mr. Ponder."

William snickered. He'd spied on the kissing game my friends and I had been playing at the last ice-cream sociable our church gave. The only reason he hadn't tattled on me was because I had threatened him with bodily harm if he did. I was still taller and bigger than he was, though dealing with him now that he was eleven was getting to be more and more of a tussle every month that went by. No matter, when the time came that I couldn't whip him anymore, I would outwit him.

After that Mr. Ponder kept quiet, and I think everybody must have dozed in spite of the coyotes and owls and moon—except for his horses. By the watch Mama kept pinned to the bosom of her dress, it was nearly midnight when we got to Switzer Wells. Mr. Ponder called out "Whoa" to his horses, then to us, "We're here, folks."

I hadn't been impressed with Leacock, which after Saint Louis seemed a town of wooden shacks trying to look like a town. But Switzer Wells hadn't gone even that far. It was a bunch of squarish buildings that looked to me to be made out of mud.

"They're sure funny-looking houses," came from William.

"They're made out of adobe, Sonny," said Ponder. "That's bricks made out of mud. The kind of houses the Mexicans build."

"Well, at least they are houses—not Indian huts." Mama seemed on the ragged edge. She asked, "Where are we to stay?"

"The Casa del Rey." Ponder pointed to the left side of the one street. "It's the biggest place."

I looked where his finger was aimed. It didn't strike me as being much bigger than the others, and it looked just as dead asleep as the rest of the town. "What does the name mean, Mr. Ponder?"

"The house of the king."

"Some king!" sniffed William.

"It's a joke. The family that owns it is named King. They take in paying guests. It ain't as if a lot of people come here to Switzer Wells."

"What keeps the town going?" I asked.

"Some silver diggings a couple of miles from here and a turquoise mine."

Now that was interesting to me! One of my Ness relations in Massachusetts owned a necklace of turquoise beads. So this country was where turquoise came from!

We drove up to the Casa del Rey, and Mr. Ponder got down from the wagon to lift first Ann Viola and then Mama down. William crawled over to the back seat and dropped their carpetbags down to them. Then Mr. Ponder led them across a sort of porch under a row of posts to the front door and knocked.

After a while a lady with a lamp in one hand stuck her head out. She had a wrapper on and her hair in one long black braid over her shoulder. "*Sí?*" She asked. It was a question.

"Señora King, it's Malachi Ponder from Leacock." He had his hat off to her. "Can you take in two lady wayfarers out of the night?"

"*Sí,*" she said, opened the door wider, and let Mama and Ann Viola inside.

Then back came Mr. Ponder to climb up onto the driver's seat. "Nice lady, Señora King," he told us, as he turned Victor and Treasureen around. "She's a Mexican," he added. "Not like that ornery King—and not like that cussed whelp of his."

"Whelp?"

"Yep, little old Jess King. That kid is pure poison

let me tell you. Jess can cuss the hinges off a barn door."

I wasn't too worried when I learned Jess, whoever he was, was only a child. A boy who was that sort of person wouldn't take any interest in Mama and Ann Viola.

Mr. Ponder told me next, "Look ahere. Why don't you get in back with your brother and try to get some shut-eye, little lady? It's quite a piece from here to Leacock."

"Thank you. I will." I got over the seat without any help, not even caring if the tops of my boots showed. This wasn't a country where a person should try to stand on her dignity. Not after what we'd been through in the last two days! I made William, who was half asleep, move over and then I slept too. But before I went to sleep I felt inside my dress for the gold piece I had put there wrapped in a handkerchief. Mama knew I had it with me. It would pay for William and me to live in a hotel in Leacock until Mr. Ponder sold the Nomad. I wondered if Arthur, whoever he was, had started to unload it already.

William and I got our first look at Arthur the next morning about nine, but Arthur didn't see us until later. He'd got the hotel off the flatcar all right. The boards and canvas were on the ground beside it. So was the furniture—a batch of shabby chairs, knocked-down tables, and two sofas, a red one and a purple

one. Arthur, who looked to be about twenty-five or
so, was sound asleep on the purple sofa with a rifle
lying across his lap. I'd got the notion that he might
be white like Aunt Natalie, but he was a pure Apache
by the looks of him.

On the way into Leacock Mr. Ponder had explained
that every Apache in his own tribe or band seemed
to be a cousin of every other Apache. He'd also told
us that Owen had never once been allowed to talk
to Natalie while he was courting her.

This had dumbfounded me all right. "How did she
ever know that he was in love with her then?"

"Oh, Natalie knew. All ladies jest know when a
man's smitten with them." Mr. Ponder surely talked
strangely at times. I had it figured out that he'd been
out West for so long that he used Western expressions
and mixed them up with some Irish ones and Back
East ones. There was no telling what would come out
of his beard next in the way of conversation. "Yep,
ladies jest *know!*" he repeated.

The idea that ladies "knew" was news to me. But
I didn't argue. I figured that looking for a new wife
himself had affected Mr. Ponder's wits. Either that
or he'd gone out in the desert sun too often without
wearing his hat. He surely had romance on the brain.

He woke Arthur up with a bellow that must have
been heard by all of Leacock that had stayed behind.
"What is the good word, my boy?"

Arthur didn't jerk awake. He just opened his eyes,

then came off the sofa like a big cat, throwing the blanket off him. He wasn't dressed like the Apaches we'd seen in Boyd Valley. He had on white men's clothing, a shirt and trousers, but he had long hair and wore the Apache red flannel headband. What's more, he had on moccasins, not shoes.

"Hello, boss," he told Ponder, which showed us that he knew the English language.

Ponder gestured from the wagon at the heap of wood and canvas that used to be a hotel. "Did you have anybody coming by wanting to buy the thing, Arthur?"

Arthur shook his head.

"Not even for its wood and canvas? It could be used in other buildings."

Arthur leaned on his rifle, looking solemn. "Nobody in town to do any building. Nobody in town, boss, to sleep in another hotel."

"That's what I was afraid of." Mr. Ponder turned to me. "How about some breakfast? It's my treat. After all, your uncle fed me last night."

"Uh-huh," came from William, who added, "I guess we know what's happened to his mules."

So while Arthur went on guarding the Nomad, William, Mr. Ponder, and I went to a café where we had buckwheat cakes with molasses syrup on them. I looked carefully at the menu. There wasn't mule meat on it anywhere. I'd been a bit worried about that.

Over his second cup of funny-colored coffee, Ponder asked us, "Aren't you supposed to get in touch with some relation of yours back in Saint Louis? Some lady, as I remember?"

"Uh-huh, Aunt Willa. What does a telegram cost, Mr. Ponder?"

"Two bits if you keep it short, little lady."

I had some quarters in my purse, and I gave William one and sent him off to the railroad station telegraph office with these words of advice, "Tell Aunt Willa that we got out here safe and sound. Otherwise, she's apt to worry."

"Sure." Tossing the coin in the air, William went out into the sunshine. It was getting hot already. He was back sooner than I'd expected. "I sent it off, Damaris. Here is a copy for you."

I took it, unfolded it, and read it loud. To my horror this is what it said:

> Papa ran off to the goldfields and somebody gave Damaris a hotel. Uncle Owen is married to an Indian. Mama and Ann Viola are in Switzer Wells. Damaris and I are in Leacock with a man you don't know but who is named Mr. Ponder. An Apache Indian was sleeping on our sofa all night last night.
>
> Love,
> William Boyd

"Oh, my Lord, you didn't send all that for twenty-five cents, William?" I'd hit him later on for what he said—not now in front of Mr. Ponder.

William has a silly grin sometimes, like right then. "It didn't cost me a nickel." He took my quarter out of his pocket and shoved it over the table at me. "The telegraph operator thought it was the most interesting message he'd sent all month. He wouldn't take any money at all for it."

"I'll bet he wouldn't." I was out of my chair in a flash and running to the depot making up the message in my head that I was going to send. It read:

> Don't you believe what William sent you, Aunt Willa. He is suffering from sunstroke.

As I handed the quarter to the operator, an old man with a green, eyeshade, to pay for the telegram, he told me, laughing, "No charge, little girl. I haven't had so much fun in a coon's age as this morning. Those are really something in the way of telegrams, you know."

"Well, one of them was," I flared at him. "You don't know our Aunt Willa."

William had really fixed things. I wondered what Mama would do to him when she read the message he'd sent. Well, I had done what I could do to make matters better. I folded the copies of both telegrams

and put them in my purse along with Mr. Benjamin's
note giving me the Nomad.

You couldn't really claim that you were cooling
your heels—not in hot Arizona Territory during the
daytime. But in a way that's what I did all day, sitting
out of the sun, on the depot platform bench waiting
for somebody to come along and buy my hotel. I
wasn't speaking to William because of that terrible
telegram, and he wasn't speaking to me because I had
called him a brainless dolt, which was one of Aunt
Willa's favorite sayings. I didn't hit him. That would
have to wait until we were alone together.

Mr. Ponder wandered all over Leacock, telling
everyone he knew that there were boards and canvas
and maybe a whole hotel for sale down by the tracks.
Arthur didn't do any wandering, though. He sat on
the purple sofa with the rifle in the shade of a boxcar
that had been shunted off onto a siding too, a distance
away from the flatcar. William went over to him before lunchtime and started a conversation. I learned
when William came back two hours later that Arthur
had gone to the same school in Yuma that Natalie
had gone to. The teachers there were nuns and
priests who talked Spanish and English. Arthur could
read and write some—though he told William that
he hadn't liked school much. I'd seen from where
I was sitting that William and Arthur were getting
along just dandy. And now I knew why. William

hadn't liked school either. By crumbs, two of a kind! Arthur, who was Cuchillo's grandson, made me nervous, but he didn't seem to affect William that way.

Mr. Ponder, who smelled of liquor, brought us corned-beef sandwiches for lunch and then went off again to try to drum up a sale for the Nomad. We could get water from the well behind the depot. On one of my trips back for a drink from the dipper the stationmaster stopped me to ask, "How are you folks doing?"

"Just fine," I said fibbing. A pair of ladies in calico dresses and sunbonnets had come to look my furniture over, but they hadn't bought any of it. They'd eyed the sofas, I'd noticed, but hadn't gone near them to try them out. Arthur was sitting on one of them; William was sprawled out on the other.

Now the stationmaster said, "I see you've got yourself tied up with Malachi Ponder."

"Mr. Ponder's been very nice to us. What's the matter? Is he a robber?"

"No, it's not that."

I didn't like this man very much, so I said, "Then what is it, mister?" I hated hinting conversations.

"He's a sort of ne'er-do-well. Do you know what that is?"

"Sure I do. Our Cousin Jonah Boyd's one of those. Everybody at home says he is. He never does anything right."

"That's Malachi Ponder to a *T*. A jack-of-all-trades

and a master of none. It was his wife who kept him on the straight and narrow."

"Well, sir, at least he didn't run off to the goldfields the way everybody else seems to have done."

"Maybe he's too lazy to get out and dig."

"Or maybe too smart to want to get rich quick." I guessed that would fix the nosy stationmaster. Yet, by crumbs, I should be fair. He hadn't run off either. Some men were tending to their knitting. I decided to compliment him a little.

"I think it's a good thing that there are some men here in town in case the Indians attack."

He smiled. "I don't think you need to worry about that. The Yumas are pretty peaceful nowadays, and the Pimas and Papagos never were very warlike. Some of the Apaches still give the Army trouble, but not those around here. It's the Apaches wandering around in the desert and mountains that are dangerous—not those that come into towns. I am referring to the wild ones."

I thought of Aunt Natalie's relations. They hadn't exactly looked tame to my way of thinking—though I couldn't say I'd studied their faces, not when they turned away every time they caught me looking at them. I guessed one of the older men in Boyd Valley must be Cuchillo, but I didn't know which one he was for sure.

Because I was wary, I asked, "What about Arthur, Mr. Ponder's helper?"

"He's a good Apache, miss."

I wondered if Mr. Ponder had tamed him. If he had, that spoke well for Mr. Ponder. "Well, good-bye," I said then. "If you can think of anybody who wants a hotel, please let me know. I'll be sitting out on the platform."

On the way to the platform I asked the telegraph operator if anything had come through from Saint Louis for us. Nothing had. It was really too early to expect a reply, and maybe Aunt Willa wouldn't spend the money to send one anyhow. I looked up at the poles and copper wires, thinking of her. She'd spread what William had telegraphed her to every Boyd in Saint Louis before nightfall.

Mr. Ponder brought us the strangest dinner I had ever eaten. It was something wrapped up in a husk of corn and was very hot. It was soft, squishy, orange-colored dough inside, and what a queer taste it had!

"It's a tamale," he told me. "The Mexicans make 'em. Folks eat a lot of Mexican food in these parts. It may taste queer to start with, but it'll grow on you if you've got the stummick for it. Most youngsters have."

After we'd eaten and were all sitting around on my sofas, he came straight to the point. "Little lady, I have to tell you I couldn't turn up one single person who wanted your hotel in all the saloons I went to. Not even for its boards and canvas. You see, the future of Leacock is sort of uncertain right at the moment. The town might snap back from this migration to the goldfields, and it might not."

"I understand you, Mr. Ponder. What do you think we ought to do?"

"There's a stagecoach leaving at seven thirty. It goes through Switzer Wells. I think you and little Willy here ought to take it. It'll save you a hotel bill in Leacock."

"But what about all my stuff?" I motioned toward the Nomad.

"Leave it here with me. Do you trust me?"

I looked directly at him. I'd begun to suspect that one of his eyes might be glass; it was so hazy looking. But the other one was really true blue. "Yes, sir, I do."

"Good. Then I'll come up to Switzer Wells in five days and let all of you know what's happened down here."

"Will you bring along any telegrams Aunt Willa or our relatives back in Saint Louis send us? Or tell us if there's any news from Papa?"

"I surely will."

I took a deep breath before I said what I had to say next. It had to do with business. I'd never had anything to do with money matters before, but then I'd never owned anything bigger than a china-headed doll, a gold locket, and a five-dollar gold piece either till now. "Mr. Ponder, are you keeping careful accounts of everything we owe you? I mean, the wagon fare to Boyd Valley and Switzer Wells and what you paid out for our lunch and supper here today?"

William prompted him, "Breakfast was your treat, remember?" Bold as brass, my brother was sometimes.

Mr. Ponder chuckled. "I'm keeping track. I'll put your stagecoach tickets on the bill too."

"We want you to. We'll settle up with you later on." I was tempted to ask why he didn't buy the Nomad himself, seeing that he seemed to want to stay around Leacock, but held the question in. That would be like asking for charity. By crumbs, that wasn't *my* way of doing things!

So at seven twenty that night William and I got aboard the stagecoach with our baggage and ten minutes later rattled out of Leacock. I bashed my bones around inside the dark, hot coach for what seemed forever, though I did sleep a little bit sitting next to a skinny old man, who kept to his corner. William was luckier. He had a plump lady to sleep on, though she kept complaining and saying to him, "Keep yer place, sonny boy. Stop leaning all over me."

After six hours we were let off at Switzer Wells. The coach horses were being watered from buckets as William and I crossed the street to the Casa del Rey, which was as dark as any of the other houses.

I knocked on the door expecting Señora King to show up with a candle like the night before, but she didn't come. Instead, somebody opened a shutter and yelled, "Who are you? And what do you want?"

At first I thought this was pretty rude for people who took in paying guests. Then I decided the voice sounded like Ann Viola's, so I called out, "We're the rest of the Boyds. We want to see our mother if that's all right with you." That ought to fix her wagon.

William asked, "Is that you, Ann Viola?"

"No, it isn't. It's Frank James."

Frank James? William and I looked at one another in the moonlight.

We heard some more yelling inside the house, and then after a while the inside bolt was pulled back and the door opened. There stood Ann Viola with another girl, somebody a couple of years older—maybe William's age. This girl had on a red-striped nightshirt and the meanest, most scowling, scrooched-up expression on her face that I'd ever seen on a human head. Holding a kerosene lamp under her chin didn't make her one bit prettier. And now I noticed that Ann Viola had the exact same look on her face. She seemed straining hard to keep it, but on the other girl's face it seemed natural.

The strange girl jerked her head at our sister. "Are they who they claim to be, Frank? Do you guarantee they're the honest article?"

"Yep," came from Ann Viola, who had never said anything before but "yes." "They're my sister and brother. They aren't part of the sheriff's posse."

"Maybe they're Pinkerton detectives in disguise, Frank."

"They aren't. They're who I say they are."

The girl with the lamp stepped back. "The password around here is Deadwood," she told us. "Say it before you come in."

Because I was too weary from the long ride to argue I said, "Deadwood," and so did William. And we went inside.

"Bolt the door, Frank," the strange girl ordered Ann Viola.

After Ann Viola had, the girl who made us say a password to come into a hotel stuck out her hand for William to shake. He had the good sense to do it, though I knew no girl had ever offered to shake hands with him before. It wasn't a thing girls did in Saint Louis. They nodded or they curtseyed.

"Welcome to Robbers' Roost," she told him. Then she held out her hand to me. I took it too. She had a lot of strength—a sort of knuckle-crushing way about her. But I crushed right back and made the pressure even. "I'm Jess," she told me.

Jess? I thought back to what Mr. Ponder had said last night. He had mentioned a "whelp, Jess," who was pure poison, but I'd thought he'd meant the son of the man who owned the Casa del Rey, not a girl. But then Jessie was a girl's name, too.

Tired as I was, I was polite. "Oh, you're Jessie King?"

"Hell, no, I ain't. I used to be, but now I'm Jesse James."

William laughed right out loud, but I asked Ann Viola, "Where's Mama?" I knew Jesse James, the outlaw, had been shot and killed in April this year.

"Locked in her room," answered Ann Viola.

I rounded on her right away. "Did you do that to her?"

"Not me. She locked her door from the inside."

Little old Jess had glittering eyes—green and glittering. I figured that Mama had locked her door because of her. Well, I was not known to be a terror on two feet for nothing. "Take us to her right away, whoever you claim to be, you hear me!"

Jess leaned against the wall and asked softly in a sort of hiss, "Do you think you can make me?"

"I surely do. I can still lick the stuffing out of him." I pointed to my brother. "You tell her, William."

He said not a word, of course. He wasn't about to admit to anyone in Switzer Wells that his sister could beat him up, anymore than he'd admit it in Saint Louis.

I turned to Ann Viola. "Then you tell her, Frank."

"She can do it, Jesse. I've seen her. Don't try her out for size." Then Ann Viola muttered, "She's a tough nut to crack."

That seemed to do the trick. Jess King was staring at me with what seemed to be respect instead of measuring me with those wicked eyes of hers. I didn't even have to roll up my sleeves to show her my muscles. "Okay," she said, "come on. I'll lead the way to where we've got your mother under lock and key for ransom." And off she went down a long dark hall with the lamp.

As we followed her, I whispered to my sister, "Does she play this game all the time? It's pretty late at night."

"Jess doesn't ever let up for a minute. She doesn't give a hoot or a holler what people think of her."

That seemed quite clear to me. "How is Mama?"

"Not too good last time she let me in. The hot weather makes her sick to her stomach. I hope you've got some good news for her." I felt better. Ann Viola hadn't truly turned into Frank James, the outlaw, who was Jesse James's brother. Frank James was still alive. Jess King probably found it easier to pretend to be a dead outlaw than a living one. I'd read the Saint Louis *Republican,* too, after the death of Jesse James in Saint Joseph, which was in Missouri also. All the same, Ann Viola was enjoying being a desperate character.

I had a sinking feeling as I stopped in front of Mama's door. If she already didn't feel well, how would she take William's telegram? Telling her that we hadn't been able to sell the Nomad would be bad enough. I decided not to tell her what was in my brother's message, so I whispered to him, "William, don't tell Mama what you wired to Aunt Willa."

"Do you think I'm crazy enough, Damaris, to tell her that?"

5

SOME SURPRISE!

After I'd called out my name, Mama unlocked the
door and let us in, the three of us that were named
Boyd. Jess King was about to come in with us, but
Mama got her by the shoulders, turned her around,
pushed her out, shut the door, and locked it again.
Jess kicked a little at the door, but after a while she
went away.

"That child is a demon," Mama told me. Then she
went to sit on the bed she'd just got up out of. There
was a lamp burning on a table beside it. Mama didn't
look one bit well. "Where's Mr. Ponder, Damaris?"
she wanted to know.

"He's down in Leacock trying to sell my hotel. He
says he'll come up here for sure in five days and tell
us what's what."

"Oh, Damaris, what I'd hoped you'd tell me is that
he sold it right away."

"Well, maybe he'll sell it tomorrow, Mama."

William was his usual comfort to us. "And maybe he won't." Then he added, "Golly, it sure does smell like mud in here."

"You'd know all about that, wouldn't you, Willy?" I couldn't resist saying.

"Stop that, you two," came from Mama. "It may be mud, but it's cooler than wood. That's about all I can say for adobe, though." She got back in bed and called out, "Ann Viola, you come to bed too now!"

"What about William and me, Mama?"

"Damaris, you and he will have to make do with the floor. In the morning we'll try to talk to Señora King and ask her to find places for you to sleep. Don't expect to get anything fancy, mind you."

"I won't." There wasn't anything else to say—not after I'd seen what I'd seen of the Casa del Rey. It looked to me to be nothing but mud walls, dirt floors, and red calico everywhere else—curtains and table-cloths and Mama's bedspread. There'd been some tables just inside the front door set out in front of a wooden bar with a big mirror behind it.

William and I made do on the floor with blankets Mama didn't need and our carpetbags, with the hard and lumpy things taken out of them, as pillows. I figured that Mama and I could probably have got Señora King out of bed, but that would have meant dealing with little old Jess again. Having dealt with her once made me wonder about her father, Mr. King.

From down on the left side of Mama's bed, I asked,
"What's Mr. King like?"

Her voice came sort of muffled from her pillow.
"There's an expression used around here that fits him
to a *T*. He serves alcohol to guests who want it. I
talked to a lady today who was leaving for Semple
with her husband. She said that her husband told her
Mr. King gives away a snake with every drink he
serves."

From the floor on the other side of the bed, William asked, "What kind of snake?" Oh, that was just
like him!

"It's only a manner of speaking, William," said
Mother. "It's a way of saying that Mr. King is a rather
dreadful person."

"He's dirty as sin," Ann Viola put in all at once.
"He hasn't seen a drop of water in years. Jesse James
takes baths every other Saturday night."

Mama's words were sour. "Ann Viola, the next time
that girl bathes, why don't you suggest to her that
she wash out her mouth with soap at the same time.
Now, children, say your prayers and go to sleep. Pray
that your father is all right in this crazy country and
that our friend, Mr. Ponder, will sell the hotel soon."

We were quiet after that, but as I lay on the floor
trying to squeeze my hipbones into the dirt floor I
wondered what Frank James was praying for. I said
into the dark, "Mama, I've still got the five-dollar

gold piece Aunt Willa gave me. Mr. Ponder's putting all of our expenses on account."

"That's good, Damaris. I'm glad you kept the money. I think we're going to need it. Prices are terrible out here." She was silent for a moment, then asked out of the darkness, "Did you send a telegram to Aunt Willa as your Uncle Owen asked you to?"

Before I could answer I heard a snorting sound from the other side of the bed. It turned right away into a loud snore I didn't believe for a minute. My brother was wide awake and listening, wanting to hear what I'd say.

"Yes, Mama, we sent something off to her." I didn't tell her there'd been two telegrams, his dreadful one and my telegram that fixed things up again. If she knew there were two of them, she'd start asking questions.

The snorting began again. I reached beside my carpetbag for the book I'd taken out of it to make it more like a pillow. It was the *Ladies' Indispensable Assistant, Being a Companion for the Sister, Mother and Wife*. It was everything ladies needed to know, which is why I was studying it. It told a person how to have good manners, look after sick people, raise canary birds, cook a roast, make turtle soup and Savoy cake, the most becoming colors for blondes and brunettes to wear, and lots more. It even had a section on the management of children.

The book had very sharp corners that could be useful too. I peeked under the bed with the book poised in one hand, listening to William's snorts. Then, when I'd figured the right direction, I let the book go. It skinned past the white chinaware chamberpot that glistened in the dark and got my brother in the brisket. I saw him raise up on one elbow and shake his fist at me. But he didn't say a single word. He knew better than that. He knew that I knew how to manage children.

In the days that went by I couldn't truly say that I ever got to know Señora King or her husband. She was a plumpish, pretty lady with a white smile and quick ways about her. She needed quick ways because she did all the work, it seemed to me—the cooking and cleaning and bed making. But by crumbs, from what I could figure, she didn't have more than fifty words of the English language, and I never did figure out what they were. She was busy but nice as she talked in Spanish to her husband and to her stepdaughter Jess, who seemed to know what she said but who never told us.

Mr. King wasn't another Jesse James, though—not like his daughter. It took a lot of strength to be an outlaw, I suspected. Outlaws were always on the move, robbing and running away with their plunder. I didn't believe Mr. King had that kind of strength.

He was a sitter more than a mover. He sat all day long behind the bar downstairs and poured out whiskey for himself and for men who came inside to talk. Mr. King was a runty man. Except that he had rusty-colored hair, Jess looked quite a bit like him. He had a scrooched-up face, too. He didn't pay any heed to any of us Boyds except to scowl now and then at us from another table at meals while he picked his teeth with a gold toothpick.

We had our own table where we ate the same thing every day—oatmeal for breakfast, tamales for lunch, and beans with beef chunks or bacon for supper. There wasn't any milk—just canned milk for the coffee. However pleasant she was, Señora King wasn't much of a cook.

In the cool of the morning Mama and I walked together up and down the street of Switzer Wells for exercise. The town was less by daylight than by moonlight, when I had to admit it sometimes reminded me of pictures on stereopticon slides of Bethlehem. It had an adobe church, two stores, six saloons, two *cantinas,* which were Mexican saloons, and a black-smith's shop where horses could be rented too. It was a forlorn place. So were we Boyds—forlorn!

All of us needed baths and to have our clothes washed. Washing things didn't seem to be anything people did at Casa del Rey, though at least Señora King looked clean. Mama suspected she sent her aprons and blouses out to be laundered but didn't know where. Jess may have had Saturday night baths every two weeks, but she didn't favor clean clothes. She and her father dressed just alike—collarless striped shirts, Levi trousers, and boots. I wondered if she even owned a dress.

I took notice on the second day of our stay at Casa del Rey that Jess was truly affecting Ann Viola. My sister was going downhill fast. Mama said she was being demoralized, and I certainly agreed. Jess King wasn't a good influence on man or beast, and by the third day there I noticed something else. William wasn't laughing anymore at the James-boys game Jess and Ann Viola played. He seemed to be watching the two of them as they ran around town pretending to shoot people by pointing their fingers at them and saying, "Bang, bang." I kept count one hot afternoon while I sat in what was supposed to be the lobby of the Casa del Rey, reading my book. I was shot dead four times by Jesse James and three times by Frank. William, who was out on the porch, only got shot twice.

When he came inside to ask me to play checkers with him because he was bored, I told him, "Go on, join them. You can be Chief Sitting Bull. I've been watching you. You want to play, don't you?"

"It's better than playing with you, Damaris." He gave me a nasty look. "Why don't you play, too? You can be the Sheriff of Nottingham."

I shut my book. "That's the wrong game, William. I doubt if Jesse James King ever heard of Robin Hood or Sherwood Forest."

He ignored this piece of information and ran out of the lobby into the street where the girls were shooting at a sunbonneted lady going into the store next door. I figured Jess and Ann Viola would accept him as Sitting Bull right off, and they did. The game changed to something with more bang-bang sounds and then some Indian yells that split my ears. Mama was lying down upstairs with a headache. This wouldn't help that any, so I went up to her with a cloth soaked in vinegar to put on her forehead.

Besides I had something to talk to her about. Earlier that day she and I had had a conversation as to whether we should stay in Leacock, or in Switzer Wells nearer Owen, or go on to San Diego, or simply go back home at once. Now I said, "Mama, Mr. Ponder will bring us the money pretty soon. I think we should go back to Saint Louis just as soon as we can. If Papa comes to Boyd Valley after we've gone back to Missouri, Uncle Owen can tell him where we are. And Papa can come home, too."

"You're right, Damaris. That's what we'll do." Mama put one hand over the cloth. "My Lord, what a howling those children are putting up!" Suddenly the Indian screechings and bangings stopped, which made me guess that the three of them were eating ice chipped off the ice block in the kitchen. The railroad

brought the ice to Leacock, and a wagon brought it
to Casa del Rey three times a week under a load of
straw to keep it from melting. Mama went on, "How
I hate to face your Aunt Willa and the others back
home and have to tell them what Charlie did and
what has happened to Owen!"

"We liked Natalie, Mama."

"It isn't Natalie, Damaris. It's the fact that Owen
lives in a tepee and doesn't even really have a ranch
to speak of. They thought he was becoming a rich
man."

I sighed. That was true enough. I supposed this
was the time to speak up about the telegrams we'd
sent. But I didn't. It was just too hot. Instead, I'd go
downstairs and get a piece of ice to suck on myself
and one to fold into Mama's headache cloth later.
I was being extra nice to her. We'd had so many surprises and shocks that I felt like her myself at times.
I guessed this was what happened to people as they
got older. They started to understand grown-ups.
Grown-ups had lots of vexing problems—more than
kids did, I'd decided.

The next day Ann Viola let me in on one of Jess
King's secrets. She showed me Jess's dime novels, ten
of them. They were mostly about outlaws, of course.
And unlike the couple William used to have, Jess's
were right out in plain sight. Our teachers back home
had always said that dime novels were an unhealthy
influence on the minds of growing children.

Naturally Ann Viola was reading them in Jess's room. She seemed proud of it too. One of them she showed me was enough to raise the hair on a girl's head, even if she had a hat on. It was called *Deadwood Dick's Defiance—or The Double Daggers*. I thumbed through it, reading a little bit about Deadwood Dick, who dressed in black buckskins and ran around with Calamity Jane, who wore a big Spanish hat. Then I put it down next to a novel called *Adventures of Buffalo Bill from Boyhood to Manhood, Deeds of Daring*. I didn't even open that one. The picture on the front of it was enough to curdle my blood. It was of Buffalo Bill as a boy riding a buffalo. He had a knife raised up in one hand to stab either the buffalo or his own knee. I whispered aloud the words under the picture. "Maddened with fright, the bull bounded into the air, snorted wildly, gored those in advance, and soon led the herd."

Ann Viola said after I'd finished, "Ain't that immense, though? How would you like to be Sable Satan, Damaris?"

"Who's that?"

"Buffalo Bill's horse in the book."

"No, thank you. A horse isn't much of an offer."

"But he's a beautiful horse."

I didn't think that was much of a compliment either and told her so. Then she asked, "How about Deadwood Dick?"

"No, I don't want to play your silly game at all.

All I want is to sell my hotel and get back on a nice clean train and go home. And that's just what we're going to do as soon as we can."

"But I don't want to go back to Saint Louis!"

"You wouldn't. Ann Viola, you are turning into a hard citizen. If Papa walked in right this minute and saw how you and William are behaving, he'd give you both a good talking to with a bed slat. When Mama and I go back to Leacock in Mr. Ponder's wagon after we get the hotel cash, you'll be going with us if I have to tie both of you to the seat hand and foot."

First she stuck out her tongue. Then she stuck out her finger at me and said, "Bang, bang, Sable Satan." Finally she glared murderously, looking quite a bit like Jess King.

I walked out, leaving her glaring. I had better things to do, such as sitting out on the porch hoping for a cool breeze while I kept watch for Mr. Ponder. Our money was being gobbled up fast by staying here so long. I was starting to worry the way Mama was worrying. Papa had left us in a fix, and Uncle Owen hadn't been any help at all. It looked to me as if Mr. Ponder was going to have to be our salvation.

Six days later I had started to mistrust him. Had he run off with my hotel or had he simply run off, maybe to the goldfields, too? He didn't show up when he was supposed to.

Finally after I'd gnawed my fingernails up to the first joint of my fingers, he came. It wasn't any promised five days since we'd left Leacock on the stage. It was a full ten days. I'd wanted to telegraph him from Switzer Wells. The line was repaired by now, according to the storekeeper next door. He worked the instrument in his store, though there were seldom any messages coming through. I didn't, though. I was afraid that nagging from me would make Mr. Ponder angry, and that wouldn't do at all.

And now, by crumbs, the man had arrived at last. He showed up real early one morning. From inside the Casa del Rey I heard his voice yelling "Whoa" as I was getting up. I scooted to Mama's room to get her out of bed. Then I pushed her window open to look out onto the street. With our heads in it, Ann Viola couldn't get hers out to see. She pinched me cruelly on a tender spot so I kicked backwards with my bare foot at her. I wasn't in any mood for her games.

This was one of the important moments in my life!

It was also one of the biggest surprises I ever had. Mr. Ponder hadn't come with just one wagon. He'd come with *five* of them. Four of them were pulled by mules. Those mule wagons were flat ones, but right now they were loaded down with boards and canvas.

Lord in heaven, he'd brought my hotel here with him! It was the last thing in the world I wanted to see. And I wasn't one bit interested in the cow that was walking along tied to the back of wagon number five. It wasn't a beef cow. It was a milk cow! What on earth!

But the hotel and the cow and the five wagons weren't the really big surprise. Mr. Ponder had something else with him. I couldn't believe my eyes. Neither could Mama. I saw her clutching at the window-sill, then heard her cry out, "Ann Viola, bring me my spectacles immediately."

"You don't need them, Mama," I told her. "You're seeing what I'm seeing. Yes, it's Aunt Willa!" Oh, to get my hands on William and wring his neck. This was the work of that telegram he'd sent off.

I told Mama, "I'm more dressed than you are. I'll go meet Aunt Willa." Mama was still in her night-gown. She'd been having trouble sleeping, because there'd been some noise out on the street last night, a burro braying. I planned to head Aunt Willa off and explain the telegram William had sent before Mama heard about it.

So I ran out of the room and stood on the porch waving at Aunt Willa, Mr. Ponder, and Arthur, who was driving the second wagon. "Good morning," I called out.

Aunt Willa was the first one to speak up. She turned to Mr. Ponder and prodded him with the handle of her parasol. Her voice rang out just the way it had in Saint Louis as she told him, "My dear sir, aid me to get down from this vehicle of yours." And now she stood up. Aunt Willa wasn't a small lady. She wasn't very wide, but she was built quite tall. As a matter of fact, she was taller than Uncle Owen or Papa or Cousin Jonah or most of the other Boyd men. They hated that. She had dark hair going gray and dark eyes, a long face, and the bulging forehead, but she wasn't a get-rich-quick person. Not her. She had a no-nonsense brain, and she looked like what she was—even in the wilds of Arizona Territory—a Saint Louis lady. Her linen duster wasn't very wrinkled. Her black bonnet was straight on her head and her jet-beaded purse firmly knotted over one wrist. Her dark blue silk parasol was in her other hand.

After Mr. Ponder had lifted her down, she came straight to me on the porch. "Damaris, where is Lucy? Where are your shoes?"

"In her room, Aunt Willa. How are things in Saint Louis?" I held my breath.

She let out a sniff of disgust. "How could they be after those dreadful telegrams you and William sent to me?"

"*Me?*"

"Yes, you, Damaris. Your telegram on top of his alarmed everyone greatly. We thought William was dying of sunstroke, thanks to you. I decided to come out here on the train as soon as possible." She shoved me ahead of her into the Casa del Rey, saying, "Now, Damaris, tell me. Where is your father?"

"We still don't know."

"Dear Lord! Where is Owen then?"

"Where we left him, in Boyd Valley. His wife isn't really an Apache. It can all be explained. William just got mixed up." Now I saw Jess King coming out of the kitchen. She crooked her finger at Aunt Willa and went "bang," then ducked back inside.

Aunt Willa ignored her. She was too busy looking over the tables and the bar of the Casa del Rey and sniffing the air. "It smells of mud in here."

"Adobe does. Aunt Willa, why did you come out here? Did the family send you?" I was standing my ground in front of her, something I'd never done before.

Usually she hadn't paid a lot of attention to me except on Christmas and birthdays, when she did her duty by the family, but now she noticed me. She towered over me and said, "That oaf of a Ponder says that you, Damaris, have clear title to the hotel he's brought up here. Is that true? Do you have a legal paper that says so?"

"Yes'm. It's in Mr. Benjamin's own handwriting."

"Excellent. I'll examine it later."

I asked my question again. "Did the family send you, Aunt Willa?"

She tucked her parasol under her arm. "No, they didn't. It was my own idea. At first I came out of my Christian duty to rescue you from my brother Charles's folly and to bring you safely home. Mr. Ponder informed me in Leacock that those horrible telegrams you sent were true in a way, though not quite so bad as they sounded. I have brought some money with me to buy return tickets for all of us. I decided that if Charles has deserted you, we should desert him as he deserves to be deserted."

"Mama wants to go home, Aunt Willa!" This ought to please my aunt. She wouldn't have to argue with Mama about going.

"Lucy *would*. That's the weakling Ness blood in her for you." I hadn't pleased Aunt Willa with what I'd said at all. There was scorn in her words. "Damaris," she told me, "things have altered a lot since I set out from Saint Louis. Now I know about your hotel and have seen it, though I can't say I approve of the manner in which you got it. And on the train out here I overheard a very interesting conversation some railroad men were having in the dining car. They thought I was only a silly female traveling out to visit relatives so they talked freely in front of me. I simpered at one of them and let him think he had me pegged correctly."

"What did they say?" Asking her this might put her off the track of the telegrams. I didn't think that mine had been so bad.

She sounded triumphant as she whispered in my ear, "Keep this secret, Damaris, if you know what's good for you. There's to be a spur of the railroad built from Leacock to Switzer Wells and points beyond. This odd hamlet is going to boom as you would never believe. The railroad people will try to buy up as much land here as they can—and rather soon, I suspect."

I didn't truly understand all of this, but what she'd learned from eavesdropping seemed to tickle her. I'd noticed already that grown-ups' eavesdropping was quite all right. It was only children who weren't supposed to do it.

She went on, "I think it's perfectly splendid that you have the Nomad."

"You like my hotel?"

"I do, Damaris. What all of us need now is a very cool head at the helm." She even smiled at me. "Child, I see real opportunities here that could easily be of more benefit to me than working as a part-time and unpaid bookkeeper for the Boyd family. This is a new land. There could be room for a *woman*'s talents here! Now where is your mother?"

I couldn't say a word by this time, but I could still point. Aunt Willa sailed past me down the hall and past the three Kings without even nodding her head at them. While I was still looking after her, thinking about what she'd said and remembering that she didn't like working for her oldest brother, the man who was Jonah's father, Mr. Ponder came up to me with her carpetbag and leather satchel. He was quite red in the face, but he was grinning. I guessed he might have strained himself lifting her down out of the wagon. I had heard him grunt.

As he put her baggage down on the floor, I asked him, "Mr. Ponder, you couldn't sell the hotel for me?"

"Nope, little lady. I tried hard, but nobody wanted it." He didn't sound one bit sorry about it to me.

"Why did you bring it up here then?"

"Because of your aunt."

"What's Aunt Willa got to do with it?"

"She has decided to put it up."

"What?"

"You heard right, little lady." Mr. Ponder had a misty, faraway look in his good eye. "By the powders of war, that lady can twist the heart of a man."

"*Aunt Willa?* You mean *Aunt Willa?*"

"I surely do. She's become a partner of mine—a business partner, I mean, though I could wish for a warmer relationship."

"She's your partner, Mr. Ponder?"

"Yes, sirree, I've got two partners now."

"Who's the other one?"

"You are, little lady, you are."

"*Me?*"

"Yes, sir."

I was struck dumb in my tracks at that moment. *I* was about to go into business?

There was a strong odor of bay rum about Mr. Ponder. It was nicer than the whiskey smell he'd had that day he'd tried to sell the Nomad for me in Leacock saloons. Probably that day he'd been just about the only man in the saloons, but I suspected he'd had a drink in every one of them. I wondered about the bay rum. To smell that sweet after traveling for hours in the desert he must keep a bottle handy in the wagon.

He sighed and told me now, "Yes, sir, that Miss Willa's a daisy, isn't she?"

I knew what that meant all right. A boy in Saint Louis had called me a dandelion once when I'd hoped he was going to say a daisy. He'd had some mean ways about him. Mr. Ponder's calling Aunt Willa that told me the whole story. By the seven sleeping sisters he'd fallen in love with Aunt Willa.

And without consulting me at all, he and my aunt had decided to set up in the hotel business, in my hotel. My boards and canvas. I supposed I should have been grateful that they were making me a partner, but I wasn't sure.

I was about to tell Mr. Ponder that the hotel belonged to me and not to Aunt Willa—and certainly not to him—but I clamped my jaws shut on the remark. I needed money. And I was a minor. Both of those things could be very troublesome, I'd learned since I'd come out to Arizona Territory.

By crumbs, I was kerflummoxed again.

6

"UP SHE GOES!"

Aunt Willa was with Mama for quite a while before
they both came out to breakfast. Mama looked rather
distraught, which was a word she favored. It meant
that she thought she was going out of her mind. I
guessed our aunt had told her about the telegrams
and the coming of the railroad and setting up the
Nomad. That would be a lot for anybody to take in
at one time. And Mama must have told her about
Uncle Owen and Aunt Natalie—if Mr. Ponder hadn't
explained it all already. Mama, as I said, looked distraught as they came out to get their morning coffee,
but Aunt Willa looked pleased with herself. I guessed
why. She'd seen Mr. Benjamin's note. Mama had
sent Ann Viola out to get it from me.

Aunt Willa even smiled at Mr. Ponder over her
oatmeal and soft-boiled egg. Señora King had boiled
an egg for her, probably because she demanded it.
None of us had ever dared. Little old Jess had told

107

William and Ann Viola that her pa and she had first call on any egg their hens laid.

I took notice that Mr. Ponder hardly ever took his eyes off Aunt Willa. Once he let go of a spoonful of oatmeal, and it dripped down the front of his vest. When I mopped it off for him, he didn't even seem to notice. He was besotted with Aunt Willa all right. It surely had happened fast. I wondered if she knew, the way ladies, according to him, were always supposed to know when a man was in love with them.

Then Aunt Willa and Mr. Ponder got up to go see the mayor of Switzer Wells, who was also the storekeeper and postmaster and telegraph operator next door. Because they insisted that I go along with them, I knew it was a business matter. I also knew enough to keep my mouth shut when Jess asked me as I went to get my hat why Mr. Ponder had fetched all those old boards and trash up from Leacock. She couldn't see a hotel when it was right under her nose. All she saw was canvas and boards. The furniture was hidden from sight in a wagon that had high sides to it.

Cleverly I told her, "Who knows what Mr. Ponder will do next? Who else would bring a cow here?"

"That's a fact. And he's got a fierce Apache savage with him," she added. "My eagle glance is set upon that Indian." I was sure that sentence had come out of a dime novel.

"Oh, Arthur! We know him," I said to her. "He's

not one bit savage. We know his whole family. They're fine people." I didn't know if Cuchillo and his band were fine or not, since they wouldn't even look at us. But they hadn't attacked us, and they let our uncle marry a lady they considered an Apache.

What I'd said left Jess looking a bit goggle-eyed as I went to join Aunt Willa and Mr. Ponder, who were waiting for me. I walked past Arthur. He'd had his breakfast on the porch because Indians weren't allowed inside. Mr. King's sign nailed to the front door said "Indians keep out!" Arthur could read, so he hadn't come inside to be humiliated.

I stopped and told him softly, "This won't happen in my hotel. You won't have to eat out on the porch there."

I'd expected a smile, but I didn't get one. Yet he didn't look away from me. "No," he said. "I won't eat outside there. Waiters eat in kitchens." Then he surprised me by asking, "What does Damaris mean?"

I knew all right, and I hated it. Damaris was in the Bible. The name means "calf," which is "little cow." Oh, well, he could look it up, too, if he could read signs saying to keep out, so I was honest. "It means 'calf,' Arthur." Changing the subject fast, I asked, "Were you ever a waiter?"

"In Yuma, yes, Rising Moon."

Rising Moon? Apache waiters? These were two new ideas thrown to me all at once. Well, I could see what Arthur might do around my hotel to earn his keep, and I liked the name he'd just given me better than Calf.

Now Aunt Willa called to me, and as I left I wondered what Arthur called her. And Mr. Ponder. I suspected Arthur still had a lot of Indian ways.

My partners in the hotel business wanted to see the storekeeper to find out who owned what land in Switzer Wells. I already knew from hearing Mr. King talking. For the most part, the storekeeper, who was named Mr. Baynor, owned the town's real estate. He'd been the first person to settle there. Oh, he'd watched the Nomad arrive. It had been the most interesting thing to happen in the whole month. But he didn't recognize that it was a hotel on wagons the way Mr. Ponder had spotted it on the train.

Mr. Ponder was canny, it seemed to me, as he talked to Baynor. "We want to buy a little piece of land to put up a coupla tents so Mrs. Boyd and her kids can stay here till her husband comes from the goldfields and takes 'em all back home. It has to have a well on it."

Aunt Willa chimed in. "It's too expensive for them at the Casa del Rey. And heaven only knows how long they'll have to wait for my brother Charles Boyd to get here."

"Boyd? Any kin to Owen Boyd, are you?"

"He is also my brother."

The storekeeper laughed. "He's a pretty famous character in these here parts, let me tell you." That remark let me know what I'd already suspected. Not many men in these parts had married an Indian.

Aunt Willa gave Mr. Baynor a look that could turn a waterfall into an icicle. "What do you ask for a piece of land, sir?"

"Where do you want the land, ma'am?"

"At the edge of town, the edge nearest the road from Leacock, so my sister-in-law and her children won't have to walk so far in the heat to come here to your store."

He nodded. "It'll cost you twenty dollars there for a parcel of land with a well on it. It's cheaper at the other end of town. Only ten dollars a parcel. I've got property for sale at both ends. Folks who used to live on the properties dug wells on both of them. There's water hereabouts, but you have to work down to get it."

"Mr. Ponder, give him a twenty-dollar gold piece," ordered Aunt Willa, "and get a bill of sale for the property." Then she asked Baynor, "Can I send a telegram from here?" She was smiling at him. She'd foxed him properly, and she knew it.

I watched Mr. Baynor push a piece of paper and a pencil over to her. "Just you write it down, and I'll send it off right away."

I stared at the big jar of peppermint sticks and smelled the fresh-ground coffee as Mr. Baynor wrote out the bill of sale and Aunt Willa penned her telegram.

By crumbs, I didn't know why I'd been forced to go with them unless it was to make it all legal because I was the third partner. Third? I ought to be first. The Nomad was mine. I planned to get Mr. Benjamin's note back from Aunt Willa, who hadn't returned it, just as fast as I could.

When we were outside and the telegram had gone clicking on its way, Aunt Willa showed me a copy of the message she'd sent. "Here's another for your absurd collection, Damaris. This message I am sending makes sense at least."

I didn't think it did. It read:

Dear Boy. Come at once to Switzer Wells, A.T., and bring the brown satchel in my closet with you.

"Aunt Willa, who's Dear Boy?"

"Jonah. He's searching for a business opportunity, too."

"But he's taking care of our house and our dog and cats, Aunt Willa!"

"The young man who is boarding with Jonah can do that."

"He's taken a boarder—in *our* house?" This was news to me. I wondered if Mama knew, but if she didn't Aunt Willa could tell her.

Aunt Willa took me by the arm. "Now, Damaris, don't you breathe a word of this to your sister or brother or anyone else. That land I paid a double eagle for will be worth two thousand dollars at least when the railroad comes here. Everyone in this mud town could become rich if he plays his cards correctly."

I thought of Papa, who hadn't, and I went from that thought to Mr. Benjamin's note. "Aunt Willa, I'd like my note about my owning the hotel back, please."

I could tell this didn't sit well with her, but she hauled it out of her purse and handed it to me with the words, "You'd best give it to your mother at once for safekeeping."

"I will." Mama could put it into her little Bible.

After giving Aunt Willa a melting look out of his good eye, Mr. Ponder went off to pay the wagoners and have the Nomad unloaded onto our land. Aunt Willa swept past Arthur, who hadn't moved from where he was squatting against the wall on the front porch. She got shot at by Jess before she made it through the front door of the Casa del Rey, but she took no notice.

While I was being aimed at by Jess, I asked Arthur, "What do you call Mr. Ponder?"

"El Boss. He pays me."

I nodded. That made good sense. Next I wanted to know, "Do you have an Indian name for Aunt Willa, too?"

"Big Winter Chief." Then he said, reminding me

that I hadn't asked about the cow, "Mr. Ponder says
the cow's name is Brown Betty." He nodded sagely.
"Betty Butter is what I say." Now I knew why they'd
brought a cow—for butter and milk in my hotel.

"I like the name Rising Moon, Arthur. Thank
you."

And then I went inside too.

After we had the land, things moved pretty swiftly.
Two of the men who'd brought my hotel to town
stayed to help put it up.

Mr. Ponder, or maybe it was Aunt Willa, had
thought of most everything, including Brown Betty.
William had been put in charge of her and getting
hay for her from the livery stable in town. He admitted he liked cream on his oatmeal, but he didn't
take to the cow. We paid little heed to his complaining. Other things were much more interesting.

One of the wagons was loaded with kegs of new
nails to put the Nomad together, which showed that
someone had truly thought ahead in Leacock! That
had to be Mr. Ponder, who had been a carpenter.

At sunset, when it was cooler, I went with William
and wandered through my furniture, which had been
set out on the ground. Arthur was on the red sofa
this time, while the two wagon drivers who'd stayed
behind were on the purple one eating suppers of
beans Aunt Willa had brought to them out of the
Casa del Rey. I didn't know why it took three men

to guard the Nomad. I guessed Mr. Ponder and Aunt
Willa weren't taking any chances with someone stealing the lumber. Not when they considered my hotel
a traveling gold mine.

Mama wouldn't have allowed my furniture in our
attic at home. It was horrible, scratched up where it
wasn't torn or burned by cigars. The upholstered
things had stuffing poking out and scarred arms. I
counted fourteen mattresses, so I guessed the hotel
must "sleep" fourteen people. They were a sight,
lumpy and sagging, and they had burns in them too.
The best-looking thing I had was a big black cookstove trimmed with shining nickel. And it was something no hotel guest would ever see. Bosh! Now that
I was looking my hotel in the mouth I thought I
could see why Mr. Benjamin had wanted to get rid
of it. It could be a white elephant—a very shabby one.
I wouldn't have stayed in it if it had been set up in
Saint Louis. No, sirree!

I hoped Mr. Ponder and Aunt Willa knew what
they were doing.

The next morning William and Ann Viola and I
were on hand to see the hotel go up. Of course, Jess
King was there, too, still being an outlaw, but everybody was too interested in the Nomad to play with
her. Ann Viola even told her straight out, "Keep
quiet, Jesse. It might turn out to be a bank." I'd
threatened both my brother and sister with bodily
harm if they told anyone that this was a hotel, not

a couple of tents for the four of us. Switzer Wells would have to reckon with its second hotel soon enough. I felt in my bones that the Kings wouldn't like the idea.

Mr. Ponder was very dramatic about the first nail used. I couldn't see why. The board the nail was being driven into had nine other holes in it already and appeared to me to need a coat of whitewash in the worst way. All the same he shouted out as he bashed the nail with a hammer, "Up she goes." It was a wonder he didn't hit his finger, because his eyes were on Aunt Willa, not on the nail.

He knew what the Nomad looked like, because he'd been inside it before. He thought he could recall how the rooms were supposed to be set up. Although he didn't have any sketches on paper, there were markings on the boards and canvas that he and one of the wagon drivers figured out.

Aunt Willa trusted Mr. Ponder, but I wasn't sure that Mama did. In her heart, she didn't want to go home without Papa. I could understand that. I thought I could read her mind even deeper than that. She was afraid he wouldn't ever come back. This new country was dangerous. All Mr. King ever seemed to talk about to the men at his bar was people who'd been killed by Indians, people who'd died of thirst in the desert, which was all around Switzer Wells, and people who'd been bitten by rattlesnakes.

That kind of talk hadn't made Mama and me feel one bit easier about Arizona Territory and Papa's safety. Being a fine whist player wouldn't be much help to him where he was now.

By crumbs, I would never have believed that a building could rise up out of a pile of boards and a heap of canvas so fast. They had it up in two days' time, and the third day they put the boards together that made up the beds and moved the furniture inside.

Mama and Aunt Willa and I brought water to the men while they worked, and we unpacked the two big crates one wagon carried. We hoped that they would contain the hotel's blankets and sheets and crockery. We were doomed to disappointment. There weren't any sheets or pillow slips, and the blankets were a sorry sight, stained and ragged. There weren't any dishes at all to eat from. My "crockery" was chamber pots and basins and pitchers for the bedrooms, all of them chipped. There were tin forks, spoons, and knives, though, most of them bent out of shape, but they could be straightened.

Nobody understood why there weren't any plates, so while Mr. Ponder was resting on a nail keg Aunt Willa and I went over to ask him. She said, "What on earth did people eat from in this place?"

He laughed up at her. "As I remember, most of the plates were tin ones. Because of the nail in the middle, they must have buckled when the tables were taken down and the hotel got moved on to the next town.''

Nails? Nails in the middle of tin plates! Come to think of it, there had been a lot of nail holes in the tops of the tables.

I said, "Nails?"

Mr. Ponder nodded. "Yep, Mr. Benjamin had a dandy system going for him. Folks who came to eat at the Nomad when I had grub there were pretty tough nuts for the most part and in a big rush, too. So Mr. Benjamin nailed the plates to the table. After a gent had finished his beans and bacon, a waiter wiped the dish with a wet rag for the next man who wanted to eat a meal.''

"Merciful heaven!" That was the first time I'd ever heard Aunt Willa say those words. She didn't call on heaven often. She believed God helped those who helped themselves.

"Benjamin didn't do that with the coffee mugs, though," Mr. Ponder added.

Aunt Willa didn't laugh the way I did. She said, "We are traveling back to Leacock tonight to buy chinaware.''

"Tin would do better, Miss Willa," he warned her. Then he smiled. "Yes, ma'am, anything you say, partner." He stared admiringly after her as she walked away, and he said to me, "That fine woman could be the death of any man. How many duels have been fought over her affections, I wonder?"

I knew the answer to that. Not one duel, but I wasn't about to say so. Yet she was supposed to have been the death of one man. He was one of my uncles, the next to the oldest. She'd been his bookkeeper, and she'd worked him to an untimely grave. He used to say she should have been born a general in the U.S. Army.

In a way I pitied Mr. Ponder. Aunt Willa knew he was crazy about her. I'd heard her tell Mama, "That oaf of a man would jump through hoops of fire if I snapped my fingers and told him to."

Once it was up, the Nomad was so big that nobody in Switzer Wells would believe that it was just a temporary home for the Boyd family. Its bedrooms were tiny boxes on dirt floors with canvas walls and ceilings, but there were twelve of them. And there was a lobby and a dining room and a kitchen and even an outhouse out back. There had been boards for that, too. The outbuilding had one side for "Ladies" and another for "Gents," but because Mr. Ponder had told me once that there were a lot of folks in the Territory who couldn't read English I'd bought some paint at Baynor's store and painted pictures on the doors. A lady with a parasol on one and a man in a plug hat on the other. That was my contribution to the hotel that belonged to me, and it was an important one in my estimation.

The Kings came over to visit us the afternoon we moved in, which was just after Aunt Willa and Mr. Ponder and the two wagon drivers had started back to Leacock. Mr. King knew by now that we had the second hotel in Switzer Wells, and he didn't like it. He didn't say so in English, though he talked to his wife in Spanish a lot as they walked around, inspecting. Señora King gave Mama and me a sad look and that was all. Then the two Kings went back home.

Little old Jess stayed to speak up for the family. She had something to say to every one of us.

To Mama, she said, "You have abused our hospitality." That wasn't fair. We'd paid for our beds and food at the Casa del Rey, and we'd paid plenty.

She told me, "You, Sable Satan, are a snake in the grass." I guessed I must have been included in the game after all.

Then came William's turn. "Sitting Bull, you were the first redskin I ever trusted, and you have proven yourself false and treacherous."

She saved Ann Viola to the last, and she pointed at her. "Frank James, you have stabbed me, Jesse, your own flesh-and-blood brother to the heart. I shall take vengeance upon you. You will tremble with mortal fear. I will send the plagues of Egypt down upon you."

"Oh, bosh," I told her straight out. I knew from

Sunday-school lessons what the plagues of Egypt were. There had been a lot of them, things like hunger, floods, insects, and millions of frogs. I couldn't see that Jess King could do anything like that. She couldn't send us a flood because there wasn't a river anywhere nearby. She couldn't starve us out or order flies and fleas to come after us, though there were plenty in Switzer Wells. As for frogs, there wasn't a frog pond for miles around so far as I knew!

"Bosh," William told her, too.

Ann Viola said only one word, "Jess—"

"Yes, a plague of Egypt!" Then, little old Jess stabbed her finger first at Mama, then me, then William, and Ann Viola. "Tremble, all of you!"

After she'd gone, Mama said wearily, "I would never have believed that girl had ever been to church in her life, would you?"

7

A MESSAGE
FROM THE INTERIOR

I was lying in bed that night in the room I was to share with Aunt Willa, thinking about Papa, when all at once I saw the canvas being lifted up over my head. There was a lamp lit in Mama's room across the way, and her door was open to get some breeze. So I had light to see by.

Because I was scared, I sat up in bed and as I did, I saw a hand come into the open place. I recognized that hand right away because it was so small, and though it was dark brown with dirt at the moment, I still knew that it belonged to little old Jess. Not scared anymore, I reached up to grab it and give her the fright of her life, but she pulled it back before I could get hold of it.

I bidded my time, trying not to laugh. She was making swear-word sounds outside now, and I supposed spying on me through a big knothole in the sideboards that only went shoulder-high in my hotel.

Well, I'd fix her. I started to throw back the blanket that was over me to hurry to the knothole I'd forgotten to plug up with a cloth, station myself alongside it, and stick my finger in her eye when she peeped at me again.

But I didn't get there in time. Jess surprised me—not me her.

The canvas was lifted up again, and this time she pushed a bucket through into my room with both of her hands. She tipped it over fast, and what was in it was thrown down onto the top of my bed.

Lizards! Three lizards. Big gray-brown ones at least a foot long apiece. One ran up the board wall behind me, another went down the blanket onto the floor over my toes, and the third one headed directly for me. I grabbed at its tail to swing it around and toss it off my bed.

And then a horrible thing happened that I couldn't believe. The lizard's tail broke right off in my hand, but the lizard kept coming at me. I let go of the tail, which went on thrashing around, and got the lizard behind the head, but that was a mistake, too. It turned its head backwards, opened its mouth, and clamped its jaws onto my hand. The bite hurt, and it hurt even more when I jerked the lizard off me with my other hand. It didn't want to let go and bit me deeper.

With my hand bleeding, I jumped out of bed and ran into the hallway yelling, "Help, help, there are lizards loose in the house!"

Then things really got wild in the Nomad. Jess King had made the rounds with her bucket of lizards. While I was standing shrieking in my nightgown, William came bolting out of his room with a lizard that must have been sixteen inches long running tailless in front of him.

Next Ann Viola came rushing out of the room she and Mama shared. There was a smaller lizard behind her. She ran up to me and flung her arms around me and tried to climb up me. When she caught sight of my bloody hand, she screamed, "Mama. Mama. Damaris got bit. She's going to die of lizard bite!"

Mama didn't come out at all. And when I understood my sister's words, my stomach fell down to my insteps. I might be poisoned to death. I saw that William's face had gone as white as Ann Viola's.

"Mama, Mama!" I howled and made a dash for her room.

She'd fainted dead away in bed. There were two dropped lizard tails twisting themselves into and out of circles on her blanket, but no lizards to be seen. The canvas over her bed had been pulled back too.

Then, Lord be praised, Arthur showed up. He had a lizard in each hand. Both of them were squirming and turning around trying to bite him. Neither lizard had a tail. He took one look at Mama, walked over to the open place, and threw the lizards outside.

Ann Viola pointed at me. "One of them bit her. Is she going to die?"

He shook his head. "Not poison, not like rattlesnakes. Lizards can bite pretty good, though, huh?"

"But they drop off their tails!" my sister cried out. She was shuddering and sobbing now.

"Don't worry. The lizards grow them back. You scared 'em bad."

I wasn't one bit concerned about the lizards—only about myself. But at least he ought to know if I had been poisoned or not. I'd take his word for it. He was a native in those parts. I'd wash the bite, put a cloth over it, and go back to bed and hope that we wouldn't have any more plagues of Egypt. I figured Jess had settled for lizards because frogs weren't available. But first I'd get Mama awake. So I burned a feather from her hat in the chimney of the kerosene lamp, and the horrible stink of it did the trick. She came out of her faint. While she was still in the fainting spell, William and Arthur had brushed the tails off the blanket and under the bed. The way they kept on twitching was enough to give anybody the willies.

I knew what Mama's first words would be, "Children, I shall fill an early grave." They were, too.

We couldn't agree on what sort of revenge we ought to take on Jess. Make her eat the tails or beat up on her or tell her stepmother. Ann Viola seriously suggested that I should go over and bite her. We didn't do anything, but we kept William on guard watching the Casa del Rey by day and Arthur watching by night.

It wasn't as if we were open for business yet. We didn't have dishes, so we bought a few for us at the store and some canned food, too, with my five-dollar gold piece. Mama's money had all gone to pay our bill at the Casa del Rey.

Mr. Baynor was very interested in our setting up a second hotel in town. While Mama was picking out some canned fruit, he came up to me and said, "Well now, little lady, you people must think you can make a go of another hotel here or you wouldn't have put it up." He had a foxy kind of grin on his face as he added, "That Malachi Ponder and that Miss Boyd aren't anybody's fools, if you ask me. Maybe they've got some information that nobody else in town has?"

Aha! He was trying to pump me, a child, for information. Not personal information. Business information. I was thrilled. People had tried to pump me for family secrets for years. This was different—honest to goodness, grown-up, man-to-man pumping. Truly flattering. So I told him, "Mr. Baynor, didn't you know that I am a partner in the Nomad?" That would show him who he was dealing with.

He gaped at me. "You, little girl?"

I nodded. "As a matter of fact, I am Partner Number One, you know." I reached into my memory for what the right words were and found them. "I mean I'm the senior partner."

Mr. Baynor's eyes bulged, but he didn't say anything more to me. He knew that I was not to be

pumped or trifled with. He'd find out about the railroad coming when everybody else did. As it was, with
him owning most of the property in town, he was
going to become a very rich man in short order. I
didn't intend to put it in his way to get rich quicker
by raising the prices on us for what he was going to
sell us.

Aunt Willa, who brought back the dishes and
other things we needed two days later, was disgusted
by the story of the lizard attack and wanted to know
if little old Jess had struck again. When I told her
no, she agreed with me that it would be very difficult
to carry out plagues of Egypt without a nearby river
and that probably Jess had only the one plague up
her sleeve.

Mr. Ponder laughed about it. He said that the
lizards were desert lizards, sometimes called alligator
lizards, and hard as the devil to catch. We knew that
but wondered along with him how Jess had caught
so many. Maybe she raised them behind the Casa del
Rey as secret weapons.

Our Cousin Jonah thought the whole thing was
"simply immense." Oh, yes, they'd picked *him* up
at the depot in Leacock along with satchels and va-
lises and carpetbags—and the special brown satchel
Aunt Willa had asked for by telegram. It had money
in it—which was what I had expected—her life sav-
ings.

I didn't mind the money, which was always a good thing to have around, but I minded Cousin Jonah. I had never taken to him. He was nineteen, tall and skinny, and trying to grow a black mustache. He looked down his nose at a person who was younger or not as well dressed or who didn't use words as big as he did. He was the scholar of the family. At least, his nose was always in a book when there was any work to be done. All of the men Boyds had tried to employ him but had let him go. It seemed to me that Jonah had been turned out to pasture as a colt.

And now we had him. And Aunt Willa, too! Both bad pennies, as I saw it. I wished I had a lizard left over to drop down Jonah's back and bite him, but they'd all disappeared. Today Jonah was wearing a pale gray suit, a pearl-and-silver-colored brocade vest, and a gray derby hat. I could see how elegant he was through the coat of yellow Arizona Territory dust all over him. He even had a cane with a gold head.

I showed him his room, being glad that there was nothing in it but a bed and a chair and table. Not even a mirror. He'd have to fiddle with his skimpy mustache without being able to see it. Hurrah!

"Maybe later on," I told him, "when we start having guests stay here, William will move in with you and share your bed. That'll free another room for a guest."

"William?" He wrinkled his nose at me.

"Or Mr. Ponder—or Arthur." That'd get him. I'd

seen how he'd stared at Arthur. It wasn't the sort of normally curious look anybody from Missouri would give an Apache Indian. It was a look that had said "savage Indian."

Because of that I told him, "Be careful around Arthur, Jonah. Apaches have been known to slit a person's throat if they aren't well treated." That ought to make him step nicely and politely around Arthur and later on around Natalie and her rela-tions—if they ever came visiting. Somehow I didn't think Uncle Owen was very eager to have her meet Willa and Jonah. If he found out they were out here, too, he'd probably stay in Boyd Valley. Well, as far as I was concerned, there wasn't a lot to choose be-tween the three of them. They were all "painful people."

After I left Jonah unpacking his carpetbags and muttering because there was no chest of drawers or closet or wardrobe, I talked to Mr. Ponder in the lobby. "Is there any new news about the railroad coming here?"

"No, but I trust the word of your Aunt Willa that it'll be coming. She's a daisy all right."

"Yes, Mr. Ponder, she wouldn't make a mistake when she set out to eavesdrop." I wondered if he was courting her in earnest yet. So I asked, "Did you have a nice trip by starlight down to Leacock?"

"We surely did. We talked all the way about the plans we have together."

"Oh?" After all, as a business partner I had a right to be nosy.

"About this old hotel." Changing the subject without telling me what I should be knowing, he asked, "What's your opinion of your Cousin Jonah?"

"What's yours, Mr. Ponder?"

"He's too citified yet for these parts."

I snorted. "Too sissified, you mean? He's a snob. He reminds me of a camel the way he looks down his nose at me, and I'm his cousin."

Ponder chuckled. "You know, he does at that. He looks like every other camel I've seen around here."

"Around here? Camels! Here in Arizona Territory?"

"Yes, sir, there are some still around, left over from the days the U.S. Army tried to use camels as transport animals like the Arabs do in the desert over in Europe."

He was wrong about his geography. There weren't any Arabs in Europe, but I didn't correct him. Grown-ups hate to be corrected by kids. So I went out to the kitchen where Mama and Aunt Willa were taking the dishes out of a barrel filled with sawdust. I asked Mama, "Did you know that there are camels out here?"

"No, but I know about snakes and scorpions and, my Lord, do I know about lizards! Damaris, if you told me that there are fire-breathing dragons two miles away, I'd believe you. This is an accursed country."

"Oh, tush, Lucy," came from Aunt Willa. "It's the land of opportunity for anyone with grit and a strong back and arms and a willing cow that's a good milker." Brown Betty was, too, or else she liked William. She gave lots of milk. My aunt turned to me. "Damaris, get a bucket and when we're finished unpacking here, spread this sawdust over the floors of the dining room and lobby. That way the ground won't show through so much, even though nobody is going to be deceived that we have a rug. We want to make the Nomad as pleasant as possible for guests, even if all we have to serve them at first will be beans, bacon, and canned goods." She held up a finger. "But there will be cream and butter. That will attract customers who don't like canned milk any more than I do. Not to mention that dreadful canned butter!"

She turned back to Mama. "Lucy, would you believe that perfectly ridiculous Mr. Ponder hinted marriage to me on the way to Leacock? Or, at least, I think that's what he meant when he said that he and I ought to work out 'good in double harness.' I told him that she who travels fastest travels alone."

I asked, "Aunt Willa, why don't you and Cousin Jonah go visit Uncle Owen and his wife and let them know you're here too?"

She snapped at me, "Never! I have no wish to see

Owen and neither does Jonah. I have heard that Owen tried to borrow money from you when you were there. Knowing him, I suspect he'd say hello to me and then try to borrow the cash I have just as he did from you."

That took care of that. I'd rather hankered to see them together, Owen and Willa. That would pay them both out a little bit. After all, he'd been the one to urge Mama to send a telegram to Aunt Willa. He was the real cause of getting her out here, and he wasn't suffering one bit because of it. I'd like to ride out to Boyd Valley with her and Jonah and see them eat mule meat, too, without knowing it.

So I went back to Mr. Ponder, who was still taking his ease on one of my lobby chairs. "Mr. Ponder, may I talk to you, partner to partner?"

"Sure, sit down." He invited me to take one of my chairs, so I did. Then he said, "I have a suspicion you want to talk about your charming auntie, don't you?"

"No, I want to talk about my charming uncle." I came straight to the point. "Maybe Uncle Owen has heard from Papa. After all, Papa knows where Owen is and not exactly where we are."

He looked thoughtful. At least, his forehead was wrinkling. "That could be true. We checked the telegraph office in Leacock before we left, and there weren't any messages for your mother."

"Perhaps there aren't any telegraph wires yet where Papa is?"

"That could well be. I'll go out tonight." He asked me, "What do you think of our place now?"

"Not much, Mr. Ponder. Not when the wind that's too hot to breathe without singeing your lungs in the daytime blows dust through the boards and lizards drop on a person in bed and there are scorpions ready to sting you on the floor."

"Well said, well said. Just the way my poor Maude used to say it. She longed for snow."

"Who doesn't?" We were going to buy ice from the same wagon that brought ice to Casa del Rey, but it hadn't come up yet this week.

"I don't want snow. I left Pennsylvania because of it and Indiana because of it and Texas because of it. Cold weather is not my pleasure."

Well, he *was* going off to Boyd Valley, so I had settled my present business with him. Because I'd said all I had to say and wasn't in the mood to hear a lot of love talk about Aunt Willa or more about snow, I went out onto the front of my hotel to look across the street at the Casa del Rey. There sat little old Jess on the shady porch in a chair, her legs pulled up under her. She was scowling at me. She was barefooted and in her Levis while I was in petticoats, a long skirt, tight bodice, apron, stockings, and boots. This surely wasn't the climate for elegance. I wondered how Cousin Jonah would work out in the Territory? Just thinking about him made me grin to myself.

Little old Jess thought I was grinning at her. She got up and shook her fist at me and yelled, "Curse you, Sable Satan. You are an inhuman scoundrel."

I called back to her, "Sure I am. Sable Satan's a horse. A horse isn't human. What did you expect, you dunce?" And I went back to the kitchen to inform Mama that Mr. Ponder was going to visit Uncle Owen and Natalie. I was absolutely certain that Ponder would be going alone, unless Arthur accompanied him.

He did go alone and came back the day after around noon. But there was somebody with him, a boy about my age, sitting next to him on the front seat under the canopy. He was an Apache, dressed like the Apaches in Boyd Valley.

"This here's Mahkto," Mr. Ponder told me, jabbing his thumb toward the boy. "Owen says he's a good hand with horses and can help out with odd jobs. All you got to do is teach him English."

I rummaged in my memory. I'd heard the name Mahkto before. Yes, he was the one who'd temporarily ruined the telegraph service to Switzer Wells by climbing a pole for the glass on it to make earrings for Natalie. I figured out what had happened easily. Natalie and Owen were getting rid of Mahkto and shoving him off onto us. I had a good idea that the Boyds back in Saint Louis were tickled to death to have Willa and Jonah off their hands, too. My white elephant was attracting human white elephants!

I told Mr. Ponder, "If he's going to work for us, you'd better tell him to leave the telegraph poles alone or Mr. Baynor will get angry."

Ponder nodded. "Mahkto's been told that already. We've got to keep on the right side of Baynor because he sells us grub, don't we? At least, until we can get freighted food off the railroad. That's another reason for having Mahkto here. We'll need some fresh meat. He and Arthur can hunt for us."

"Hunt what, Mr. Ponder? Coyotes or owls or snakes or jackrabbits?"

He shuddered. "Not jackrabbits. Deer and quail like I told you—and javelina. That's wild pig."

Wild pig didn't sound tasty to me, but it wasn't anything to turn my nose up at, not after I'd eaten mule. I longed for green turtle soup and roast goose and lemon ice.

Mahkto took the wagon around behind the Nomad after Mr. Ponder had got down from it. I asked Ponder, "Has Uncle Owen heard from Papa?"

"He surely has." He smiled at me showing his own gold mine. "Fetch your mother, and I'll deliver the package to her."

"A package?"

"Not much of one. It's more like a half of a handkerchief." And now he pulled the dirtiest-looking piece of cloth I'd ever seen out of his shirt pocket.

"Mama!" I hurried to the kitchen, where Mama

and Ann Viola were doing the breakfast oatmeal
bowls. They were being washed in pails of water,
because we didn't have a pump in the kitchen yet
or a sink.

"What is it, Damaris?" Mama turned around, looking weary. She was also very put out, and I couldn't
blame her. Jonah had complained about the lumps
in the oatmeal.

"Mama, Mr. Ponder's back. He's got a message
from Papa that Uncle Owen had."

"Why didn't Owen bring it here himself?"

"I don't know. Ask Mr. Ponder."

So I led the way to the lobby with Mama and Ann
Viola trailing me. Mr. Ponder held out the piece of
cloth to Mama. "Here, dear lady."

"What on earth?" She sat down, holding the filthy
thing, staring at it. It was all knotted up. She looked
at Ponder. "Are you sure this is from my husband?"

"Owen says it is. An Apache on his way to the
Colorado River brought it to him two days ago. The
Indian was a cousin of Natalie's. He told Owen that
the cloth was from his brother—Owen's brother, I
mean—and that it was for his squaw. That's you, Mrs.
Boyd. I don't mean any disrespect. That'd be the
Apache way of putting it."

Mama sniffed. "Yes, I know some Apache ways already." She began to work at the knots, but they were
so tight he had to undo them for her.

Inside the cloth there was a piece of paper that

looked to me to be the twin of the one Mr. Benjamin
had given me in Spar City. Mama unfolded it while
we waited, but she didn't read it aloud. There was
something else in the note. A little piece of metal
that was yellow. It gleamed in the palm of her hand.
Mr. Ponder whistled. "By the powders of war,
folks. He's gone and done it. That's a gold nugget.
It's a handsome one, too."

"Gold?" Mama said the one word softly and, I
thought, sadly, too.

"What does Papa say?" I asked.

"All right, you might as well hear the whole thing,"
she told us. Then in a hoarse voice she read it, turning it over and over to read along the edges.

Wednesday, (I believe?)

Dearest Wife,

Because the place where I am has no name yet,
I will only say that this is a message from the in-
terior, if that makes any sense to you.

We have had a little success here in the diggings and have staked out what could turn out to
be a rich claim, my partner and I. He is the same
Mr. Benjamin you met on the train.

I am sending this nugget to you in care of
Owen, because I know you went to him. I am
sure that he was able to help you and look after
you.

Mr. Benjamin believes that there could be

great possibilities in this gold camp. He has seen
a great many of them. He advises us to sit tight
here and make our fortunes.

So I think that you and the children should
return to Saint Louis. When I have recouped
our fortunes, I shall come back to Saint Louis,
once I have visited our land in Boyd Valley and
seen Owen and his bride.

Take care of yourself and the children, Lucy.
I send my love to you, each and every one, and
Mr. Benjamin sends his best regards. Put your-
self in the capable hands of Willa back home.

Your loving husband,
Charles

P.S. The nugget is to be sold to buy train tickets. I found it the first day here. I trust finding
it wasn't just beginner's luck. Mr. Benjamin
thinks that I am a lucky sort. This is why he
invited me to be his partner.

I couldn't help saying, "Papa surely was lucky to
Mr. Benjamin on the train!"

I saw Mama lift her eyes to the sagging ceiling of
gray canvas that was the ceiling of my hotel. This
time she didn't say, "I shall fill an early grave." She
said, while she tore the handkerchief to shreds, "He's
in the hands of that human hyena, Benjamin."

"But he did find some gold," Mr. Ponder told her.

"And you're already in the hands of Miss Willa, ain't you? Your husband'd be comforted if he knew what was going on around here. You folks going into business, I mean."

"I am not at all comforted, Mr. Ponder." Mama put the letter in her apron pocket along with the nugget. "I am furious. I'm going to find Willa this very instant and show her this latest evidence of the family disease." She stamped her foot and out she went to the place Arthur had made for Brown Betty. Aunt Willa was learning to milk a cow in what was an Apache wickiup, though she didn't know that was what Arthur had made.

Using my head, I sat down next to Ann Viola across from Mr. Ponder, who was looking pretty surprised at Mama's sudden leaving. He probably didn't think she had sand enough in her craw to get mad enough to stamp her foot. But I knew how mad Mama could get. She didn't have any intentions of obeying Papa and going back to Missouri. No, she wasn't going to sell the nugget to buy train tickets. It appeared to me that we were in for a long, hard haul. By using our heads we could make life in Switzer Wells a little easier.

So I told Ann Viola, "Go over and make friends with little old Jess. Be Frank James if she wants you to, even if we have to forget about all those lizards of hers. One plague of Egypt is enough. Remember there were ten of them, and she could have a pretty good imagination because of those novels she keeps on reading."

That afternoon Mama, who hadn't wept once, ordered me across the street to Mr. Baynor with a telegram to go to her Massachusetts Ness relatives. They would have been waiting to hear from us and maybe worrying by now.

Because I was sending it, I had to read it. This one said:

We are flourishing, running a hotel here in a beautiful community called Switzer Wells. Regards to everyone at home.

Your Lucy

Two days later Mama got a reply that said:

So happy that you and Charles are flourishing. Do be careful of the savage Indians. Lily has been disappointed once more. Love from,

Mother and Father Ness

I gave the copy to Mama, and after she'd read it, I asked her, "What has Aunt Lily been disappointed in?"

"Love, Damaris. Bosh! Lily doesn't know how lucky she is to have escaped marriage." She put the paper in her apron pocket and stalked off to the

kitchen, where she and Aunt Willa and Arthur were
making butter.

I followed her. Making butter was more interesting
than making talk with Mr. Ponder, though churning
the cream to make the butter come was mighty hard
work.

I couldn't say much for the telegram from Massachusetts, but one good thing had happened that day.
The ice wagon arrived from Leacock, and we'd
bought ice, which we put into a big metal tub in
the kitchen. The ice would keep the butter fresh
after Arthur churned it, and chunks of ice would
cool the buttermilk that was left after the butter
came. There was nothing to beat ice-cold buttermilk
on a hot day! I'd better enjoy drinking it while I
could. Aunt Willa had told me that when we had
guests at the Nomad the buttermilk and butter would
be for them, not for us if we were going to make a
good profit.

8

WE MAKE
SOME PROGRESS

Mama was a changed woman. Everybody noticed it, but Aunt Willa was the one to explain why a week later. She told me one night while I was darning some of William's stockings after supper and Mama was on the other side of the lobby talking to Mr. Ponder. "Always remember, Damaris, that getting angry and doing something about being angry is an excellent tonic for a woman."

"Yes, ma'am." I was already tired of Aunt Willa's giving orders to everybody all the time, but I agreed with her here. Ladies didn't have to suffer in silence any more than men did. So I said, "Mama isn't going to give up the ship either." Yet I doubted if Mama had it in her nature to become a terror on two feet.

Aunt Willa, who was scratching away on what was going to be our hotel desk, adding up how much money we'd spent outfitting the Nomad, looked at me over the tops of her spectacles. "That's the ticket,

child. Say 'no' when you want to. Ladies don't have
to sit back and accept just everything that comes
along in life. Sometimes a lady has to back up her
opinions with some forcefulness." Here she positively
glared across at Mr. Ponder.

I guessed why. He'd talked to her some more about
pulling in double harness. I'd heard her tell Mama
this, and I'd been of a mind with Mama that it certainly wasn't a very romantic way to propose marriage. I supposed that came of his having been in the
livery stable business, though he'd sold out in Leacock, according to what he said. It could lead a man
to thinking in horse language, being around horses
all the time.

I was about to tell Aunt Willa that I agreed with
her when all at once Ann Viola and Jess came running inside as fast as they could, streaking toward
the back of my hotel. They made a breeze as they
went by, but it didn't last long enough to comfort me.

"Head for the hills, brother," Jess was howling.
"We'll ambush the black-hearted fiends at the pass."

I couldn't exactly say that we were friendly with
the Kings, but Ann Viola hadn't had a lot of trouble
taking up with little old Jess again. There weren't
many kids their age in Switzer Wells. The Mexican
girls were too ladylike for them.

Right on the girls' heels William and Mahkto came
running in. My brother and he had hit it off together
right away, though Mahkto didn't speak English yet

so far as I could tell. Because of Mahkto, William had stopped being the Sioux Indian chief, Sitting Bull. After all, he had a real Indian to play with now—and a boy, too. Like me, William had received an Indian name from Arthur. It was Wild Horse Hunter. I didn't know what game the two boys were playing with Jess and my sister, but they seemed to be chasing them a lot of the time. I suspected it was outlaws being chased by Indians.

As the boys thundered past making more noise than the girls, I yelled at Aunt Willa, "When do you think we'll be opening for business?" I was getting tired of waiting around. It wasn't any fun being the senior partner in a business that wasn't doing any. We hadn't had one single guest in the Nomad yet. The two people who'd come by stagecoach to Switzer Wells had been people the Kings already knew, so naturally they had stayed at the Casa del Rey.

Aunt Willa waited until the boys were out of earshot. Then she told me, "Mr. Ponder's going to Leacock tomorrow night to see what he can find out." She sighed, something she rarely did.

I knew why. She'd had some words with him recently. He wanted to serve alcohol in the Nomad. She didn't. She was a member of the Women's Christian Temperance Union in Saint Louis, and the whole reason for their organization was to stop people from drinking liquor. I had looked the word *temperance* up in the dictionary and found that it meant something like not too much of anything at one time, but the ladies in the Missouri WCTU didn't want any liquor sold legally in the whole United States. As far as I could see, it wasn't temperance they were after but abolition. Well, it didn't concern me. I was a minor. Nobody asked me my opinions on anything, though the hotel was really mine. I was getting less and less pleased at *not* being asked too.

I suspected Aunt Willa would win out over Mr. Ponder. Love had weakened him. He was a changed man, it seemed to me. There was a sort of decayed look about him these days. He'd even given up dousing himself with bay rum, because he was losing hope or he'd run out of the stuff. Or maybe he'd drunk it up! I had a good idea where he'd try to find out whatever he could about the railroad coming to Switzer Wells down in Leacock. First, the depot and then every saloon and *cantina* in town. After that, he'd sober up before he came back here. Aunt Willa had made it very clear at the supper table what she thought of men who drank.

"Rotten sots," is what she called them. So Mr. Ponder couldn't sneak over to the Casa del Rey for two reasons: because Mr. King was mad at us and because Aunt Willa might catch him doing it. If she caught him, that would be the end of his courting her. In her younger days she'd slipped the mitten to two men who'd wanted to marry her when she found they drank "ardent spirits." Oh, the Boyd men didn't go along with her notions. They pretended she wasn't there at holiday dinners and oyster sociables when wine was poured. Nobody even put out a glass for her.

I put down the stocking and went over to Mama. "Shall I get Ann Viola and William and the others out of here for you?" They were making a terrible ruckus.

"No, Damaris. At least I know where they are when they're creating an uproar. If they keep up all that noise much longer, though, please ask Arthur to tell Mahkto to quiet things down." Arthur was out behind the hotel smoking a cigar Mr. Ponder had given him.

We had all noticed something interesting. All Arthur had to do was say a couple of Apache words, and Mahkto behaved himself. I figured that must be another Apache way. I wished I had the secret to use on William. I thought Mahkto was a sort of mysterious person, and not only because he didn't speak much English. We couldn't get him into any of William's clothing. He was wilder than Arthur, I had decided, though I couldn't put my finger on what it was about him.

After I promised Mama that I'd fetch Arthur inside if things got too much out of hand, I spoke to Mr. Ponder. "Aunt Willa tells me that you're going to Leacock tomorrow night."

"That I am, little lady. Is there anything you want from there? A doll maybe?"

By crumbs, I didn't like that remark. "I never did play with dolls." That was a fact. In that respect I was a bit like Aunt Willa. I didn't melt into jelly at the sight of some lady's baby any more than she did. I was tempted to tell him that I would like a bank in Switzer Wells and another store and a hand laundry but didn't.

He took a better tack next. "Partner, I want to talk some business with you."

I told him, "Mr. Ponder, anything you have in mind to say you can say in front of my mother."

"All right." I noticed that his good eye was somewhat dimmer than before, misty looking, as a matter of fact. He spoke very softly, "Your Aunt Willa, she's a dumpling, ain't she?"

I knew what he meant. That went along with being a "daisy." I told him, "Beauty is in the eye of the beholder." Thinking about his argument with Aunt Willa about selling liquor, I went on, "A woman likes to have her way in some things, you know."

As far as I was concerned personally, I'd decided that the Casa del Rey, which was smaller than the Nomad, could serve whiskey, and we wouldn't. We Boyds would set a good table and have clean beds. That ought to be enough as I saw it.

That railroad spur couldn't get to Switzer Wells

fast enough for us. There was trouble brewing here. Right now I needed both of my partners. Even if I was the senior partner, I wasn't quite fourteen yet. Oh, I was learning and learning fast, but I had a ways to go in business. I'd given up one idea already: that Mr. Benjamin had cheated Papa. That had been Papa's fault, not Mr. Benjamin's. It had been a noble gesture on Mr. Benjamin's part to give me his hotel. I didn't know how it was going to work out, but I was willing to give it a chance.

Mr. Ponder asked me, "What does that wonderful woman, Willa, think of me?" Was this his idea of talking business? What it really was was pumping!

Right out in front of Mama, who was frowning warningly, I said, "Aunt Willa doesn't confide much in me yet, but if you are a partner of hers, I guess she must respect you." Now while he was grinning and in a good mood, I asked him for the favor I'd been wanting for six days, ever since the notion had come to me one Sunday morning at dawn while I was listening to the King rooster crowing across the street at the Casa del Rey. "Mr. Ponder, I'll tell you what Aunt Willa says about you from now on if you'll do something for me."

"What would that be?" He bit hard.

"Teach me how to play poker, please." I looked out of the corner of one eye at Mama, expecting her to go right through the canvas ceiling. But she didn't even twitch. She looked resigned more than anything else.

By her expression I knew that my promise to tattle on Aunt Willa had pained her, but all she said was, "I think, Mr. Ponder, it would be a good thing if someone in the family knew something of that game, other than what we learned on the train coming out here."

I thought he was looking very hopeful as he asked her, "Are you saying that you're going to have a gambling hall in here, Mrs. Boyd?"

"No, I certainly did not say that, Mr. Ponder." Mama got up and went over to Aunt Willa to talk. A couple of minutes later both of them turned their heads in his direction to glare at him. Then they went out to the kitchen. Mama had good reason to hate gambling. Permitting me to learn the game of poker was for our future protection. I understood that. Still, I thought that poker should be interesting to know, though I didn't see how I was going to use this knowledge in Saint Louis where the Boyds played only whist.

Mr. Ponder was gone for five days, and then on what had to be the hottest, driest July morning I'd ever had to live through he showed up. He brought exciting news with him. He'd learned from the telegraph operator in Leacock that there were some railroad men, bigwigs, in town. He told Aunt Willa and Mama and me very proudly, "Yes, sirree, I played my cards close to my vest with them gents. I stuck like glue to 'em hoping to overhear something they'd have to say about Switzer Wells. It took me three full days of trailing 'em around town. But one night one of them let something slip."

"Where did that take place, Mr. Ponder?" Aunt Willa wanted to know.

He cleared his throat, betraying himself. "In a hotel, ma'am."

I knew what he was saying. In a barroom in a hotel. That's where he'd done his trailing.

She knew it, too, but wasn't about to follow it up. "Well, don't take so long about it. What did the men say?"

"That the spur line to Semple through Switzer Wells ought to be completed by the end of the month. They're getting everything ready now—the ties and rails and spikes and the crew—I reckon."

"Then the railroad men will be here almost at once?" Aunt Willa asked him.

"That's how I see it. I'm more'n likely only a coupla days ahead of 'em—not the crews that lay the tracks but the railroad bigwigs."

She turned to Mama. "Leacock people will be up here right on their heels to buy up land the minute the word gets out. They'll come here and then on to Semple by wagon."

I asked Mr. Ponder something else, "Did the Leacock men ever come back from the goldfields?"

"Some of 'em have. Not too many, though. You
know how she goes, little lady."

"We know how *he* goes!" Mama corrected him.
Nobody laughed at her joke.

I doubted if Aunt Willa had even heard her. She
was frowning. "Mr. Baynor is a smart man. He'll
know right away what's afoot when these people from
Leacock start buying up land in town. And for all
that he's the most unwashed mortal I have ever been
within smelling distance of, Mr. King is not an idiot
either." She sighed, took off her apron, and reached
for her bonnet, which was hanging on a hatrack.
After she'd put on the bonnet, she took her parasol
out of the large pickle jar we kept sunshades in. It
had been part of the equipment of the Nomad.

"Where are you off to, Willa?" Mama asked her.

"First, to Mr. Baynor's store to lay in a good sup-
ply of food before he gets the news and raises the
prices, which he is certain to do." She turned to
Ponder. "I have come to a firm decision in the time
you've been away, Mr. Ponder. There will be absolutely no alcohol served in this establishment. Once
I've done my business with Mr. Baynor, I'm going
to call on Mr. King and tell him that the railroad is
coming through and there will be plenty of business
for *two* hotels here. I am going to suggest to him that
he send his overflow of guests here to us and we shall

send anyone who wishes to drink liquor over to him. That should please the rotten sot of a man."

I saw how Ponder started to open his mouth, but she was through the door before he could get a word out. After she'd gone, he said limply, "By all the powders of war, that is a driving woman!"

I agreed and told him, "She has been known to drive people to distraction, then to drink."

I got along well enough with my aunt by never crossing her will, but sometimes I yearned to tell her the Nomad belonged to me not to her.

The Kings were friendlier to us after Aunt Willa's business call on him, but they still didn't fall all over us. Little old Jess was underfoot more than ever, though, playing outlaws.

The railroad men arrived and did their business in Switzer Wells. They were our very first guests. One of them had stayed in the Nomad in New Mexico Territory. He complimented us by saying that the place was better run by Boyd, Boyd, and Ponder than by Mr. Benjamin. The beans were better cooked, the venison and antelope Arthur and Mahkto brought in savory, the plates were real china, and the little waiter girl was "handsome as a peach." That was me! I wasn't paid any wages as the owner, of course, but I kept the silver-dollar tip one of the men gave me. It was the first money I'd ever earned. I'd worked hard for it, too. It felt good working and being paid for it,

a very grown-up, flattering feeling. I understood exactly what Aunt Willa had meant when she said she
wanted to be something on her own and not just a
Boyd family worker.

After the visit of the railroad men, it was quiet for
a week. In that time Mr. Ponder taught me how to
play some other kinds of poker besides the draw
poker I'd learned on the train. Poker games took
only one deck of cards, his, which was good because
we Boyds didn't have any. Three of the other games
certainly didn't have elegant names. They were so
inelegant I didn't tell them to Aunt Willa or Mama.
five-card stud and seven-card stud and spit in the
ocean. My favorite, though, was showdown, the game
Mr. Ponder nicknamed "sudden death." It seemed
to me to be the easiest. I soon saw that there was a
lot more to poker than just the cards. A player had
to know how to bet and to bluff. I wasn't much of a
bluffer, according to him. That took years to do well.
Mr. Ponder always won all of the toothpicks we used
in place of poker chips.

By the middle of August there wasn't time for card
games anymore. I don't think I sat down during the
day for more than a minute at a time from that date
till the middle of September. People from all over
the Territory were coming up to Switzer Wells because of the railroad. Mr. Baynor was selling land as

fast as he could, and we had all the guests we could handle. We just wished we had more rooms to put them up in.

Aunt Willa had divided up the work around the Nomad. Cousin Jonah in his best bib and tucker was the desk clerk. Mama was the cook. Ann Viola was the chambermaid, and I was the waitress, when I wasn't helping Mama and my sister. Arthur carried baggage in and out and took care of the horses along with Mahkto, who was mostly responsible for Victor and Treasureen. Brown Betty was still William's job when he wasn't helping us. Aunt Willa was mostly the manager, but she was everywhere telling us what needed to be done next. I couldn't see that Mr. Ponder did anything but be friendly to the guests. Still, he did that well, and they all said they liked our place.

We didn't use Arthur as a waiter after the first time. And because of him we didn't ask Mahkto to wait on tables at all. Someone had brought Mr. Baynor a lot of fish he'd caught up in the mountains. He'd brought them down packed in snow in a cowhide, which had kept them fresh. The storekeeper came over with two dozen of them, big trout they were. Mama put a fish aside on ice for each of us, but there were plenty left over. We decided they'd spruce up our menus, not that we had real ones. I told the guests what we had to eat at the moment, which was mostly beans and pork, game, canned fruit, pies made out of preserves, buttered baking-powder biscuits, and coffee.

The day Arthur helped me wait on table there were ten people buying up Switzer Wells property staying for supper. Fried trout went well with beans, so I told the guests that they could have fish if they wanted. All of them did.

I gave Mama the order, and because I had so many to serve at one table, I asked Arthur to serve the other. Odd! Not one of the men he served ate his trout, though they ate everything else and even wiped their plates with biscuits. I couldn't understand it, so after they'd left I asked Arthur why.

He looked right at me and said, shaking his head, "They wanted to know about the fish, so I told them."

"What did you tell them?"

"They asked if the fish was good, and I said no."

"But it *is* good! Mama said it's very fresh yet. Why did you say that?"

He explained carefully. "Rising Moon, fish lives underwater. No Apache ever eats fish. Fish is never good."

By crumbs, I'd learned another Apache way. When we had fish, which in the desert wouldn't be often, we'd hope neither Arthur nor Mahkto would come into the dining room. They would probably glower at the guests. There was something about the way an Apache stared at a person, if he looked at you at all, that was no comfort to the appetite.

I could ask Cousin Jonah to help me. He would, particularly if Aunt Willa ordered him to, but he'd act as if he was doing me an immense favor. He didn't like Switzer Wells, where burros fell asleep in the middle of the street. He laughed at the town, and it laughed at him. If there was anybody who was shot at a lot by little old Jess, it was Jonah.

I'd been wondering how she would take to the railroad arriving. She was tickled, according to Ann Viola. After all, outlaws were great train robbers, and if the town got bigger, there would probably be a bank in it, too.

One very pleasant day when it was raining dogs and cats because it was August and that was when it rained in Arizona Territory, I had a talk in the downpour with little old Jess out in front of the Nomad.

She said to me while we both got soaked, "I hope it won't be a strong bank they build here."

I didn't know anything at all about what kind of bank there would be, except that I planned to put my money in it instead of in my carpetbag bottom. All the same I told her, "I'm sure that it will be big and made out of bricks. I plan to deposit my money in it. After all, I'm in business here. You'd better not dream of stealing my money."

"Outlaws do not rob little girls," were her words.

I was hardly a little girl, but I let the remark pass. Ignoring the lightning flashes because the rain was so nice, I played the ace in the hole I'd been saving up for her all month. "If a lot more people come here to town to live, a sheriff will be coming, too."

She shrugged her shoulders. "That doesn't cut any ice with me. You'd better watch out for your ill-gotten gains, Damaris Boyd."

Ill-gotten? Running a hotel was hard work. I'd only started, and already I knew that. A person's feet ached running around in shoes in hot weather on hard dirt floors. Doing the laundry for the Nomad was a horrible chore. We didn't have sheets and tablecloths yet, but all the aprons, towels, and pillowcases Aunt Willa sent to Leacock for had to be boiled on the back of the big cookstove every night, rinsed, wrung out by hand, and pinned to the clothesline out back. I was getting more muscular in the arms not only from carrying plates of food but from wringing out laundry. I hadn't done either of these jobs back in Saint Louis, where we'd had a girl come in to help out three times a week. As far as I could see, Jess wasn't helping her parents one bit.

She looked like a soaked rat in the rain, no bigger than a minute, but mean as could be.

I waited until the lightning had flashed again and the thunder passed by over us, then I told her in what I knew was a hiss and what I hoped was dime-novel language she'd take to heart. "A gang of girls who

are outlaws isn't any better than a gang of men outlaws, Jessica Geraldine King." That'd fix her, using
her real name, which I knew she hated. "Sheriffs don't
take any more kindly to women who want to break
the law than they do to men," I went on. "There are
prisons for women. As a matter of fact, you could go
to the Territorial Prison down in Yuma if you don't
mend your ways before you commit some crime." I
pointed at her. "If you continue in your evil road-
agent ways, you will end up at the end of a rope with
a bullet through your wicked heart." Oh, I was warm-
ing up now, and I knew for the first time how preach-
ers must feel. "I warn you, Jessica Geraldine King,
you will rue and regret the course you have taken."
I remembered what I'd heard one time in church.
"Repent, girl, repent while there is still time. A
criminal is a criminal! No one is above the law of
the land!"

At that moment there was a big flash of lightning
and a mighty roll of thunder that surely put a period
to what I had said. Little old Jess was staring at me
and backing away as I went on pointing at her. At
the next flicker of lightning she turned around and
ran for the Casa del Rey, leaving me standing in the
middle of the street still pointing.

All at once, while I was feeling rather remarkable
and powerful, I heard laughter behind me. It was
Aunt Willa, who'd come out to enjoy the freshness
of the day after working inside tallying up accounts.

"Well said, Damaris, well said. Come back inside now. Your mother wouldn't like lightning to strike you, you know."

When I came inside shaking water out of my hair, she told me, "We are making some progress. There are now a few profits, not big ones, mind you, but profits all the same. We'll be getting our investment back entirely very soon."

"That's good news."

"Well, don't get too fired up about it, Damaris. We're going to have some future expenses, too, you know—new blankets, sheets, tablecloths, and, of course, a cook. Your mother can become the chambermaid then. And we must see about getting laundry service here."

"What cook? Laundry service?" I had to wait for the thunder to stop before she could answer me. She seldom yelled.

"A cook and a laundry will take time, but I do hope they come before you children start to school and will only be able to work here part time."

"School?" I hadn't thought of school at all. There was a school for Mexican children, taught in Spanish, in Switzer Wells but no public school. Jess King had gone to this Spanish school, which was operated by the church the Mexicans went to. Before she'd come to Switzer Wells she lived in a town that had had just one school, for people who spoke English.

Aunt Willa went on, "Oh, there will be a public

school, I'm sure. Parents who come here will insist that there be. A teacher will show up. When there are enough people here, I shall try to get a Methodist church and a minister and a chapter of the Women's Christian Temperance Union and found a ladies' society to press for the woman's vote in this Territory."

By crumbs, Aunt Willa didn't think small. She was unusual in another way, too. She could think in summer weather so hot I sometimes felt my poor eyeballs were becoming hard-boiled. It didn't seem to me that she even perspired.

9

ENOUGH!

The railroad work crews were within a couple of miles
of Switzer Wells by the last day of August. The next
day they laid a northbound track on the west edge
of town. Everybody in town turned out to watch
them, except for Mama and Aunt Willa, who expected railroad foremen to come to the Nomad for
dinner before they went on past Switzer Wells heading for Semple, forty miles from us.

It was a sight to see, more fun than watching the
railbed leveled by men putting rocks and gravel in
the right places. Mr. Ponder had been out to see that
chore done and advised me not to bother going.

Oh, the railroad work crews had a dandy business-
like system going! They'd brought everything they
needed with them on railroad cars that followed behind on the track they'd just put down. They'd pile
the wooden ties, spikes, and shiny lengths of rails
where they wanted them and position the ties where

the surveyor and foreman said they should go. Then four men, taking turns with sledge hammers, drove one spike after another into the tie just beside the rail itself. The spikes had been made so one edge of their heads stuck out. This edge caught the bottom part of the rail and held it firmly when the spike was pounded in.

What a clanging of hammers and shouting all of those men made! And how fast they worked, never once getting in each other's way, even though four worked together.

Mr. Ponder, who was with Ann Viola, William, Arthur, and me, yelled at me once, "Look at that, little lady. A good crew can lay from three to five miles of track a day."

I called back to him over the noise, "They're wonderful. I love to see men working!" That would fix him maybe. He'd done scarcely one lick of work for weeks, unless he called teaching me poker and talking with men guests in the lobby "work."

What I said didn't fix him, though, so I looked away from him and watched the workers. A lot of them were Chinese men in blue jackets and trousers and black silk round hats or floppy felt ones. Others were white men, mostly Irishmen, I learned later on. There were some Negroes, too. But I didn't see a single Indian.

So I called to Mr. Ponder, "Don't Indians work on the railroad?"

He came over to me. All that yelling must be a
strain, I imagined. "They don't like the trains much,"
he told me. "They call 'em 'bad medicine wagons.'
They scare away the buffalo."

I could see why Indians didn't like trains, but all
the same some Indians rode on them. Yet Mahkto
hadn't come out to see the tracks laid. Yes, he was
truly more of a wild Apache than Arthur. I guessed
that was because he hadn't gone to the school for
Indians that Arthur and Natalie had gone to in
Yuma. Mahkto hadn't always lived with the band of
Indians Arthur and Natalie belonged to. His mother,
who had died not long ago, was a member of Cuchillo's group, but he had been raised by his father's
people. Somehow I got the notion that he was only
visiting in Boyd Valley.

We had some of the railroad men stay over with us
at the hotel that night. They were nice. Though they
weren't bigwigs, they granted William the thing he
craved most of all. When the work train's locomotive
puffed through Switzer Wells heading for Semple the
next morning, William was standing out on the cow-
catcher, tied to it. On his other side was little old Jess,
who looked as tickled as my brother was, even if she
was tied on for safety, too. I thought it was disgusting
the way people cheered them. One man even called
out that they had "the brave look of our town's
flourishing future." I was delighted when the locomotive halted at the very end of the track they'd laid

yesterday and William and Jess were put off the cow-catcher to walk back home.

I figured my brother would have a swelled head, and he did until Aunt Willa informed him that a rail-road man never went out on a cowcatcher unless he hoped to snatch up a drunken sot lying on the tracks.

To my surprise as well as a lot of other peoples', that trip on the locomotive changed Jess. It was a very pleasant change, in my opinion, and in just about everyone else's, except Ann Viola's. It wasn't that Jess turned into Jessica Geraldine. She switched, though, from being an outlaw into being Railroad Rob, who, I knew from my sister, was another dime-novel hero. Now that the outlaw-gang game was dead, Ann Viola had a choice of being either Railroad Jack or Fred Fear-Not. She didn't want to be either, so she pretty much quit playing with Jess and took her doll out of her carpetbag again. We weren't shot at anymore, though Jess made us jump with imitations of train whistles, and William and Mahkto still chased her.

I changed, too, in a way a couple of days later. I stuck out my foot and tripped William as he ran by me, yelling at the top of his lungs after I'd told him to keep quiet three times already. I was getting tired of his noise. When he got up to face me, I noticed something. Arizona Territory was certainly agreeing with him. He was growing even faster. His eyes looked right into mine, and I remembered that Mahkto was teaching him to wrestle the Indian way. No, I didn't think I should fight him anymore. After all, he was my only brother. So instead of saying, "If you don't keep quiet, I'll put mousetraps on your ears," I said, "Please be quieter, William. You'll disturb our guests."

He gave me a grin that certainly didn't comfort me. It was the sort of smile that told me he knew why I didn't attack him and harm him bodily. What he said was worse. "So you ain't a female outlaw anymore either." His grammar was falling apart as fast as his clothing was.

"I never was an outlaw, William. Standing up for yourself and not getting trampled on doesn't make a person an outlaw, as I see it." I drew myself up onto my toes to become taller and went on, "I am a business lady. I work hard, and I expect to be paid what I'm worth. And I don't eat any pickles that I don't want to eat."

He came back quick as a flash. "Then why are Mr. Ponder and Aunt Willa your partners when you own the Nomad?"

He'd noticed that, too! But I only told him, "Because they had the cash to set it up, and they're grown-ups and know how to do business things."

He was still grinning at me, when I added, "Oh, go pretend to scalp Mahkto, but do it quietly."

William shook his head at me. "No, Mahkto does that. He's the Indian, not me."

"It's easy sometimes to forget which of you is which, William."

The train started running three times a week through Switzer Wells before school began. There wasn't a teacher to be had in town, which was a blow to Aunt Willa. But all the same she got one for us. She snagged one off the fifth train that passed through on the way to Semple. She got some boards, white-washed them, and then with black paint hand-lettered two signs. One was for Ann Viola to carry, one for William. They were ordered to grab the signs out of the lobby, when they heard the train whistle, and run to the train where it stopped in our town. Then both of them walked the full length of the cars. We knew some people would come to the Nomad and Casa del Rey to eat, but other passengers would have brought food with them from Leacock or Semple and would stay aboard. I was primed in the dining room to keep my eyes peeled for any lady who looked like a teacher while my sister and brother patrolled the trains with their signs that said:

Wanted—A Schoolteacher
Good Salary   Room and Board

Mama and Aunt Willa had decided we'd put a teacher up free of charge at the Nomad. They hadn't asked me what I thought and I was a bit peeved. I

wasn't at all sure I wanted a teacher living under my
roof where she'd be watching us all the time. On the
other hand, a teacher ought to quiet William down.

The teacher Ann Viola and William sadly brought
back from the train was a man, not a lady at all. He
was Mr. Wroth, a tall, thin, youngish man, who'd
come west from Vermont for the sake of his lungs to
live in Semple with his married sister. He decided
he'd rather teach school in Switzer Wells than move
in with her, because she had ten children. He made a
deal with Aunt Willa to stay with us, and Mr. Baynor
gave up the back room of his store for our school-
house. Baynor sent to San Diego for McGuffey readers
and arithmetic books right away.

Mr. Wroth was all right as a teacher, though I
couldn't say I truly took to him to begin with. He
was a disciplinarian. One glance from him at my
brother, and William hushed up. Ann Viola liked
him, and Cousin Jonah doted on him because he was
a chess and whist player. Jess King hated him on
sight. She'd hate any schoolteacher, but when Mr.
Wroth told her parents that she would have to put
on dresses and shoes, she really hated him. As for
Mahkto, being an Apache, he didn't have to go to
school. He'd go to an Indian school later, I supposed.

I was the oldest of the pupils even when some other
families who weren't Mexican came to Switzer Wells
to build stores and houses. I got a sort of spotty education because of Mr. Wroth's agreement with Aunt

Willa. He was to let me out to go to work at the
Nomad whenever the train stopped. But then I didn't
need educating as much as the others did. I had a
good head for arithmetic and was a good reader and
speller and owned the *Ladies' Indispensable Assistant.*

My, were we ever busy at the Nomad now! We ran
our feet off when the train stopped because the passengers had to eat fast, the way we had in Spar City
the day Papa ran off. I learned that it was as hard
to feed people fast as it was to eat that way. Switzer
Wells was getting to be what Mr. Ponder called a
"real boom town." We were making money faster
than we could spend it, according to Aunt Willa. We
didn't have time to do that, though she sent off to
Leacock for the linens and other things she thought
we needed to make the Nomad more elegant.

By the end of October all of us were getting pretty
frazzled. Aunt Willa, too. She was annoyed, because
she hadn't had time yet to start all of her activities
to benefit Switzer Wells. We still didn't have a church
or minister or WCTU or suffragist society.

I was more concerned about Mama, though. She
was doing too much work. She didn't talk much to
anyone anymore. There hadn't been another single
word from Papa and no men who'd been to any goldfields and come back knew him by name. I knew
Mama was pining to hear from him. We all were. And
we still didn't have any real idea of the location of the
goldfields he'd gone to. There didn't seem to be a

town out there, just streams to pan gold in and holes to dig it out of. And if there had been a town, it would be too new to be on Mr. Baynor's map. When we asked the direction, prospectors just pointed to the northeast toward some mountains.

One night the first week in November on a nice cold evening, I had a little chat with Aunt Willa in our room. Mama had gone to bed right after she'd cooked dinner and hung out our washing. Mr. Ponder was smoking in the lobby while Arthur swept it out, and William and Mahkto were in the stable. Mr. Wroth and Cousin Jonah were bent over one of the dining-room tables playing chess.

I complained to my aunt, "Nobody tells me exactly how much money we've made."

"We are doing very well, Damaris, making a tidy little profit."

I knew that was supposed to satisfy me, but it didn't. "How much? It's my hotel, remember?"

She pursed her lips, but all the same she reached under her bed for the book she kept accounts in, opened it, and showed me the figure at the bottom of the last page she'd written in. I know my eyes must have popped with pleasure. Tidy little profit, my foot! It was a lot of money to me. Two hundred sixty-seven dollars and seventy-five cents.

I said, "It's time to get a cook for the Nomad. We can afford one, can't we?"

She pursed her lips again, then said, "Well, I suppose you're right, Damaris, costly as it will be. It would ease your mother's burden a bit to have someone do the cooking. We can't have her collapsing on us. We shall set about the task."

So this time I made the two signs and sent Mahkto and Arthur out to the train with them while William and Ann Viola were in school. Mr. Ponder claimed that I had the makings of a train robber, but I didn't care.

The train was how we got hold of Mr. Wroth and how we got Mr. Toy, the cook. He was Chinese with a long pigtail down his back, and he spoke only a little bit of English. I was sure he didn't read it, but somehow he knew what our sign said.

Wanted: A Cook for a Hotel

Good Salary   Room and Board

We never found out why Mr. Toy was on the train from Semple to Leacock or where he planned to go once he got to Leacock. We never found out either what was in the straw suitcase he had with him, though we suspected it held more blue jackets and trousers and cloth shoes. He had a way about him that made you keep your distance. He bowed and smiled, but he was the king of the pots and pans in our kitchen once Mama had showed him the hotel routine the first day. If somebody came into the kitchen who had no business there, Mr. Toy would

reach slowly for the meat cleaver he used to chop
things with and mutter in Chinese. He was a truly
good cook too. By the time he was with us a month,
we were serving much better food. Even some vege-
tables and fruits! He got crates of fresh things off the
train each time it chugged through from Leacock.
We never did figure out how Mr. Toy managed that
when he didn't speak much English, but he did.
Maybe by sign language. He was very good at that.
Things like drawing a finger across his throat when
Aunt Willa snapped at Mr. Ponder. I didn't know if
Mr. Toy meant her or him, though, when he made
that gesture.

We had the old Nomad in pretty good working
order by the time the Christmas season rolled around
—our first Christmas without Papa. That was enough
to dampen it for us Boyds. We expected it to be
dreary without him, and we didn't make any real
preparations for it, though I bought peppermint
candy canes and oranges at Mr. Baynor's store for
my brother and sister and tortoiseshell hairpins for
Mama and my aunt. I got Mr. Ponder a comb for his
beard, hoping he'd use it, and a much smaller one
for Cousin Jonah's mustache, because I believed in
useful as well as ornamental gifts. I planned to give
fifty cents out of my tip money to the two Apaches,
because I had no idea at all what an Apache Indian
would want for Christmas.

I didn't know what other people intended to do

to celebrate the holiday, but on the morning of the twenty-fourth we found out what Mr. Ponder had in mind! He arranged a surprise for us, but mostly for Aunt Willa. He'd sent Arthur up in the mountains, saying he was off hunting antelope, but actually that wasn't what Arthur was after at all. He brought back an evergreen tree, which was what Mr. Ponder wanted. After Arthur had come back at midnight, he and Mr. Ponder decorated it in the lobby while we were all asleep. We hadn't thought of a tree this year, though we'd always had one in Saint Louis.

So there stood Mr. Ponder's tree the morning of the twenty-fourth. It was green all right, but that was the only familiar thing about it. There wasn't any star at the top. There couldn't be; the top was poking right into the canvas of the ceiling. There weren't glass ornaments or candles on it either. The decorations were like nothing any one of us had ever set eyes on before. Even the guests who were staying with us overnight couldn't believe their eyes.

Some of the things—lots of cigars and dull red sticks that looked to be covered with paper—were tied on white strings. There were bottles snuggled up to the trunk of the tree, whiskey bottles, some half full of whiskey, empty ones, and bottles full to the top.

The cigars we recognized, and the bottles. I heard Aunt Willa suck in her breath as Mama asked, "Mr. Ponder, what are those red things?"

Oh, but he was proud as punch, and did he ever

smell of bay rum! He must have had another bottle of the stuff. "The sticks, dear lady, are dynamite," he told us. "I tried to buy candy canes, but Baynor was out of them. Somebody bought 'em all up."

"Merciful heavens!" said Aunt Willa. "You'll blow us all to the skies."

"Not if you don't light 'em, and you'll notice that I didn't put any wax candles on the tree, Miss Willa." Mr. Ponder looked mournfully at her. "I only wanted to make you folks happier at Christmas. That's why I got the tree for you, to make you feel right at home."

"With tobacco, alcohol, and dynamite, Mr. Ponder?" Aunt Willa, who was used to bells, angels, cranberry, and popcorn chains was getting red in the face. I had never seen her that way before.

"Well, Willa, I had hoped to." He brightened. "When I was down in Leacock last time, I bought presents for everybody. I'll give them out right now."

That was just fine with me. And I was pleased until I saw what he'd bought us—orange-flower water for Mama and Ann Viola and me, and for Cousin Jonah and every other man the very same kind of pipe. William and Mahkto got big Mexican hats that didn't fit until they traded them.

Aunt Willa's present was saved for last. It came in a little tiny box. Mr. Ponder took it tenderly out of his coat pocket. I guessed what it was. So did Mama because I heard her say under her breath, "Oh, no."

I closed my eyes, hoping Mr. Ponder wouldn't do it. But he did—right in front of everybody, including two strange men guests from Semple. He cleared his throat and said, "Willa, will you do me the honor of being my bride? I promise to stop drinking and smoking entirely. I'll be your willing husband and love, honor, and respect you till your dying day." He opened the box. Yes, it was a gold band ring, a wedding ring.

I couldn't help but look at my aunt. She was even redder than before—and speechless. He seemed to get bolder because she hadn't said anything. "I am asking for your hand in marriage, Willa. There will be a preacher in town before long, and he'll tie the knot for the two of us."

At last she found her voice. She screamed—for the first time in her life, I suspected. She pointed at the ring, then at the tree, and yelled at him. "The only knot that will be tied is going to be tied by me around your neck, Mr. Ponder."

I watched her whirl around and head for her room. Mama came right after her, calling out, "Willa, Willa!" I didn't hang around to see how Mr. Ponder took being refused. Maybe he played a good hand of poker and could outbluff me, but he certainly didn't know how to court ladies.

I found my aunt bending over, hauling her carpetbags out from under her bed. She was telling Mama, "Enough! I have had enough of this town and more than enough of him. He will never give up. I know his breed of male. I am taking the train to Leacock this afternoon, and from there I am going home to Saint Louis. Thank heaven, the train comes through here this afternoon."

"But, Willa you can't. . . ." Mama started in.

"Oh, yes, I can, Lucy." She turned around, her arms folded. She was calm now. "Do you wish to come with me or don't you?"

"No, Willa." Mama sounded just as stern, but she was pale as a phantom.

"Very well." Aunt Willa turned to me. "Damaris, I shall take the money I put into this hotel and my share of the profit with me if that's all right with you. That is all I ask of you."

"It sure is all right, Aunt Willa."

"I'm sorry about this." She shook her head. "I came out here, a maiden lady, to get ahead in the world, and what did I find but that pestiferous Mr. Ponder. I simply cannot abide him another day. I ask that you tell everyone that I've gone."

"Yes, I will, Aunt Willa." Then I asked her, "What will you do when you go back to Missouri?"

"I will set up in business, Damaris. I have the capital for it now. Don't ask me what kind of business. I am not quite sure of that yet myself."

I didn't ask her. It seemed to me that I'd lost a partner, but then I'd never asked her to be one in the first place. And I wasn't about to get another one.

The Nomad was mine! Or rather, it was getting closer to being mine alone.

Aunt Willa kept to the room she shared with me until the train came, talking to Mama and me. It wasn't as if she had any real packing to do. Only her hairbrush, comb, soap, and toothbrush. In a place that didn't have closets or chests of drawers, everything stayed in a valise or carpetbag. When she sailed through the lobby, holding the brown satchel Cousin Jonah had brought with him to her, she didn't look either to the left or the right. And she didn't say farewell to anyone. She left the mattress she slept on to me, so I could put my tip money in it. It had hidden her store of gold coins. I planned to put my money in the same place until a bank came to Switzer Wells.

Mr. Ponder wasn't there to see the ruin of his hopes. According to William, he'd gone right across the street to the Casa del Rey to drown his sorrows. Cousin Jonah had gone with him. That was how Jonah took the news I fetched him of Aunt Willa's leaving. Her going drove him to drink, though whether it was because of joy or grief I wasn't sure yet. Mr. Wroth, who was talking to a man guest in the lobby, told me he didn't know either.

But he did agree with me on one thing when I said to him later on, "You know, Mr. Wroth, I don't think it was the full bottles of whiskey that got her goat or the empty ones. It was the bottles that were half full."

Mama, Ann Viola, and I said good-bye to Aunt

Willa at the train and promised to write her any news we had of Papa at once and to come back to Missouri as fast as we possibly could.

Quite a few folks in Switzer Wells saw Aunt Willa leave, including little old Jess, who didn't like her. Jess was grinning from ear to ear as the train pulled out for Leacock. Now that she was pretending to be a railroad man, Jess met and said farewell to every train that came through.

Aunt Willa's last words from the train steps were, "Don't you let Owen Boyd manage the Nomad whatever you do, Lucy!"

I called out to her to comfort her, "Don't you worry about that. *I* won't." I knew who was going to manage the Nomad from now on. *Me.* I'd get a waiter somewhere to replace me, so I could do what Aunt Willa had done.

And then just after the train pulled out, an idea came to me. Instead of going back to the Nomad with the others, I went to Mr. Baynor's store and from there I sent a telegram to Mama's youngest sister, my Aunt Lily Ness. It said:

> Merry Christmas. Mama needs you. You can come out here all the way on the train. She is weakening. Arizona Territory is just full of men that aren't married.
>
> Love,
> Damaris Boyd

I figured that said a great deal in a very few words. Mama didn't have to know what the words were, though. I knew from her that Aunt Lily had been disappointed a number of times in matters of the heart. Coming out to help us in the hotel business ought to keep her too busy to weep over her lost loves, and besides what I'd wired her was the truth. There was a shortage of single ladies out here. That was one of the chief things that the men guests who ate at the Nomad talked about. Aunt Willa had had more admirers than Mr. Ponder. As for Mama, a lot of the men seemed disappointed that she had a husband somewhere. Four of them had even asked me, "How old are you, miss?" Mr. Ponder wasn't the only man hunting a wife.

Well, he might have other troubles. I intended to have more of a say now around the Nomad. He could nurse his broken heart in his spare time. I didn't figure it would stay broken too long. I'd seen the gold ring hanging on a twig of the Christmas tree as we'd escorted Aunt Willa to the train.

As I went back to my hotel from Baynor's store, I resolved to write Aunt Willa soon. After all, I owed her something. I'd learned quite a bit about keeping accounts from her, though she had not had that in mind. I'd mostly learned from her accounts book. I wondered what kind of business she would go into in Saint Louis. It hadn't sounded as if she planned to work for anyone but herself. But there weren't many ladies who did that unless they were dressmakers or milliners. She never could sew.

Jess King was leaning against one of the porch posts of the Casa del Rey as I went by. She made a pulling motion in the air, then her train whistle sound. Finally she called out to me the most surprising words I had ever heard from her, "Merry Christmas!"

10

CHANGES

Mr. Ponder and Cousin Jonah came staggering back to the Nomad late that night to find me waiting up for them beside the wild Christmas tree. I was primed and ready to fire at them, but the sight of Jonah dried up what I had to say. He wasn't wearing his coat but had it over his arm. I saw his shirt sleeves!

He greeted me with a funny little laugh and the words, "Hurrah, hurrah, she's gone away. I peeked out of a window across the street and, sure as could be, I saw her get on the train."

"Yes, sirree." Mr. Ponder hiccupped, then he added, "I am finished with the whole race of females, Jonah, my lad. I wouldn't wed any woman alive even if she was crusted all over with rubies and her pa owned a brewery." He put his arm around Jonah and hugged him. "Don't you ever go and get tied up with anything that wears calico, do you hear?"

Then Mr. Ponder threw back his head and sang a

song I had never heard before and hoped never to hear again.

I dream of pie instead of Cupid.
A broken heart is very stupid.
I like my grub, it pleases me
Better than love or amity!

Jonah didn't join him in it. He said, "I won't, Malachi, I never will. Don't you fret. I've been under Willa's thumb or my mother's thumb all my days. And now I'm free. Liberty, sweet liberty!" Jonah had his hat on. He pulled it off and sent it to the ceiling. It bounced off it landing on a branch of the Christmas tree. He stared at me. "Damaris, what's this I see? Missy Damaris waiting up for us." He swayed as he pointed at me. "Go to bed, little girl."

I got up and told him, "You're drunk, both of you. You go to bed."

"Do you hear what she's saying, Malachi?" Jonah asked Mr. Ponder.

"I hear her, but I don't believe her, Jonah."

This got my goat all right. So I asked, "Mr. Ponder, who owns this hotel anyhow?" How glad I was that our guests had already gone to bed and didn't have to see them.

"You and me, we own it together, now that Willa's gone." Mr. Ponder was swaying too.

"So, sir, not really. Just me. It's mine, and from

now on I will make the big decisions around here."

Jonah hooted. "What decisions?"

"I intend to become the manager, Jonah Boyd. You are to be the waiter in my place."

"Waiter?" He blinked at me.

"Yes, waiter. You'll be paid wages and there are tips, you know. You'll make more money there than as a desk clerk."

"Oh." Jonah plopped down on the purple sofa. Then he nodded toward Mr. Ponder, who was admiring his unusual tree. "What will Malachi do?"

"He will be the desk clerk, and he will not be paid. After all, he says he's my partner."

Mr. Ponder swung his head around to look at me. He gave me a shake of the head and said, "All right, little lady." Then he asked, "Say, did anybody ever tell you you've got some of the look of your Aunt Willa about you?"

"No, sir, you're the first to say it." By crumbs, he hadn't meant his words as a compliment, but I wouldn't let on that I knew. So I said, "Thank you." And then I went off to bed, leaving them in the lobby. If they wouldn't go to bed, I would.

I wondered as I brushed my hair and got into my nightgown if the change in Jonah would last until the following day. That could be the whiskey in him doing the brave talking.

To my surprise, it lasted. With Aunt Willa out

of his life, Jonah was a changed man. He even shaved
off his silly mustache and bought a red-flannel shirt
at Mr. Baynor's. It made him look more like the
other men in Switzer Wells. He still played chess
with the teacher and read books whenever he could,
but now he even smoked Mr. Ponder's Christmas
pipe. Best of all, he stopped looking down his nose
at everybody and everything. He didn't have to pretend to be what he wasn't anymore, because his
mother and Aunt Willa had picked out a part for
him to play. All of us found it easier to live under
the same canvas with him. I suspected he'd never go
back to Saint Louis at all. Or perhaps he'd wait until
he'd made his fortune. There was a sort of "I'll show
you" air about him nowadays.

I understood that. I intended to show people too.
I stopped going to school at all and studied in the
Nomad in my spare time. No, sir, I wasn't going to
miss out on my education, but with the teacher living with us there wasn't any cause for that to happen.
Mr. Wroth gave me the same tests at home he'd give
any eighth-grader, and I sailed right through them
every time.

There wasn't a telegram in reply from Aunt Lily
or any other Nesses by the first of 1883, and I began
to believe that I might have peeved Mama's sister by
what I'd said in mine. A telegram did come from
Aunt Willa, though, the first week in January. It was
sent to me and said:

Arrived safely in Saint Louis. Have gone into business for myself. Please send a recent photograph of Mr. Ponder.

Fondly,
Willa B.

Naturally I showed the message to Mama, who was as surprised as I was. "Shall I show it to him?" I asked her.

"If you expect to get a photograph of him, I suppose you'll have to."

So I did. I read the telegram to him, because I wasn't absolutely sure that he could read well enough to figure it out for himself. I'd seen how he pored over the Nomad's register trying to read the names of the guests. I'd replaced him as desk clerk; it was my job, too, now. He said, "Willa wants a photograph of me?" He sounded astonished, then he smiled happily.

I tried to comfort him and at the same time not get his hopes up. "Maybe she wants a memento. At the age you and she are I doubt if many people get proposed marriage to anymore."

He gave me another look, then he nodded. "Well, if a photograph taker comes around where I am before I get too old and die, I'll get it done for her. For old time's sake. I'll send it off to her, but nothing's going to make me go to Saint Louis."

I was glad to hear that he wasn't about to go there. In time, I'd write Aunt Willa and send the photograph if we could get one, but I wouldn't write for a while—not until we had some real news.

I set about getting some news. I asked Arthur to ride to Boyd Valley and tell Uncle Owen that Aunt Willa had gone home and that Cousin Jonah was a changed man from the fop he knew in Saint Louis. Not that Uncle Owen would have known Jonah grown-up, but Jonah had had the makings of a fop even as a child, I was sure. What I really wanted to learn from my uncle was if he'd had word from Papa. I knew Mama was more worried every day that went by. One note and one gold nugget in eight months' time wasn't much to comfort a lady. I wanted badly to give Papa a piece of my mind.

Uncle Owen, Aunt Natalie, Arthur, and four strange men, all Apaches, came riding into Switzer Wells together two days later. One of the Apaches was a gray-headed man with a red blanket across his shoulder, Cuchillo himself.

How people stared at them. Indians came through Switzer Wells now and then, but old Cuchillo was someone special.

Owen and Natalie came inside the Nomad. The Apaches wouldn't, though I asked them to. They peered in through the windows and doorway. Then they squatted down in front of my hotel the whole day, and, believe me, town people gave them a wide berth. Two of our guests stayed indoors and some other men who always ate lunch at our place came

and went through the kitchen, making Mr. Toy furious. The Apaches wouldn't eat anything or talk to
us, though they talked for a time to Mahkto. Mahkto
stood in front of Cuchillo for quite a while. Standing
at our hotel desk I could see outside, and I noticed
that Cuchillo was doing all the talking.

Mama had a long talk with Owen after we'd shown
him and Natalie over the Nomad and given them a
big breakfast. I heard everything Owen told her. No,
he hadn't had any more word from Charlie. If he
had heard, he would have sent the message on to her.
It seemed to me that he was surprised to find me
managing a hotel.

He came up to me after lunch and said, "It appears
to me you've taken on a big job for a little girl."

"I'm not a little girl, Uncle Owen. How was your
lunch?"

"Just fine." He laughed, then asked, "How are you
doing here?"

"Just fine."

"I mean, are you making money?"

Oh, I knew what he was driving at. Borrowing
money from me. So I said, "We are making ends
meet." I let out the deepest, most painful sigh I
could. "Prices are very high, you know, and wages
are high too. I don't take a salary, of course, and
neither does Mr. Ponder." Never would I let him
know about the gold coins inside my mattress.

He looked disappointed. "I'd hoped you'd have some cash to spare, so I could buy some cattle."

"We don't, Uncle Owen." Then I added, "Why don't you ask Papa when you see him? Maybe he's getting rich quickly. You know how Boyd men are about that."

That stopped him in his tracks. He said, "You're quite a bit like your Aunt Willa, you know?"

"Yes, I learned a lot from her. She's got a brain for business. She told me once never to lend money to anyone. That's what banks are for. I am grateful to her for the advice."

He sighed and went outside to the Apaches.

At sunset he and Aunt Natalie and the Apaches rode away with half of the town standing out on porches watching them go. I think they felt relieved.

Afterward Jess King walked across the street to say, "It's a good thing the train doesn't come through today. If it had whistled, the Indians' horses would have run away."

"Maybe so." She'd kept out of sight all day, too, I'd noticed.

"Were those your kinfolks too?" Jess asked Ann Viola, who was still standing beside me watching the Apaches go.

My sister said, "I'm not sure if they are or not— the Indians, I mean. It's kind of confusing about them."

That was exactly how I felt. The Apaches were very interesting, but they didn't make me feel easy in my mind. I guessed perhaps Mahkto felt the same way. After he'd been talked to by Cuchillo, he'd gone out to the stable and hadn't come back yet. I could ask Arthur, who'd been with Cuchillo much of the day, what had been said, but I was so sure that I wouldn't get an answer that I didn't. Besides, it was none of my business. We couldn't afford to have Arthur get mad and leave. I needed him and every other person working at the Nomad.

But more than anything, we needed someone to help with the laundry. We had a cook, but there still wasn't a laundry in Switzer Wells, though there was plenty of water and lots of soap piled up at Baynor's store just waiting for someone to set up in business. Doing the hotel washing every night and cleaning rooms by day was wearing Mama down to a nubbin. I helped as much as I could, but I had to buy the canned food and pay wages and keep accounts, so most of the other work fell on her. Neither Mr. Ponder nor Arthur was a good hand at hanging up laundry, and, according to Mama, there had never been a man born who could use a flatiron and make a tablecloth look decent.

I wished Aunt Lily would reply to my telegram. She was not only my favorite of the Ness aunts because she acted so young, though she was thirty, she was the best ironer I'd ever seen in action. Mama claimed she was better than a French hand laundress on tucks and ruffles. My dresses had ruffles.

On Groundhog Day the train from Leacock came through and let off seven passengers. Four of them already lived in Switzer Wells. One stranger went to stay at the Casa del Rey. The other two came to the Nomad. One of them was a lanky young man with a wispy yellow beard and artistic soft black hat. He carried a big black case and valise and two carpetbags.

The second person was Aunt Lily!

I spied her first, hugged her outside, and then with my finger to my lips for secrecy brought her down the hall of my hotel to the room where Mama was making a bed. Mama had her back to us and didn't see us.

By crumbs, Aunt Lily had a sense of fun. She crept up, put her hands over Mama's eyes, and growled in what was supposed to be a man's voice, "Guess who, Lucy?"

Mama stood stock still, then she shrieked, "Lily?" I guessed it must be a game they played as girls.

My aunt let go and Mama spun around, throwing herself onto her sister, with both of them crying. When they were finished and Mama was wiping her eyes on her apron, I said, "I sent another telegram last month. This time it went to the Nesses."

"Bless you, Damaris," came from Mama.

I noticed again how much Mama and Aunt Lily resembled one another. The same reddish hair and hazel eyes and pale skin. "Fair as a lily," was what people had always said about my aunt, who was a little fairer than Mama. Aunt Lily would have to be careful in the sun out here, but she had had her parasol up when she and the yellow-bearded man had walked to the Nomad.

"I came to help you out," Aunt Lily told Mama.

Well, that was exactly what I'd been wanting to hear. I said, "It's no soft snap here, working in my hotel." She couldn't say I hadn't warned her. I added, "This is not the Southern Hotel or the Planters' Hotel in Saint Louis. Some people back there would say that a rattlesnake would be ashamed to meet his mother in the Nomad."

Aunt Lily nodded as she looked around the room made out of boards and canvas. Then she took off her hat and mantle and started to help Mama with the bed. One thing you could say about Aunt Lily, she took hold fast. But then she was a farmer's daughter! She wouldn't want to be desk clerk and manager!

Aunt Lily met the rest of my staff at dinner time when everybody was gathered together at the end of the day before we served dinner to the guests. I saw her look very surprised at the sight of my two Apaches and Mr. Toy, and she giggled. Massachusetts hadn't prepared her for them. Cousin Jonah was very polite to her, though she wasn't a Boyd. He was getting more human all the time. William and Ann Viola she already knew from last year's visit to Mama. Aunt

Lily never brought up Papa's name. I knew that
Mama had told her while they made beds what had
happened.

She didn't giggle at Mr. Ponder, though. She took
one long look at him and looked away. Oh, he had
said that he'd given up courting notions, but I hadn't
believed him at the time. Now the way he kept staring at her over his beans and hanging on to her every
word was really remarkable. I could tell by the time
the dried apple pie came around that he was besotted
once more.

And I could tell, too, that she thought he was a
poor goose of a man. After all, he must have been
nearly twice as old as she was. Later, while she and
I did the dishes, I asked her what she thought of Mr.
Ponder.

"He's an old whelp, Damaris. He's making eyes at
me like a masher. I can tell a masher when I meet
one. There's nothing in the world worse than an
elderly masher." She giggled and kept rubbing and
rubbing one plate with a towel so long I was afraid
she'd rub the gold band off its rim.

I'd hoped that she'd talk to me of her disappoint-
ments in love, but she didn't. I supposed Mama already had been told. Lady-to-lady talk. Oh well, no
matter. I was never going to allow my affections to
get out of hand and be kerflummoxed by a man the
way the two of them had.

Aunt Lily finally put down the plate and took up

a cup to dry. "What did you think of Mr. Gibson?" she asked.

"Who?" And then I knew. He was the man with the wispy yellow beard. He'd signed the Nomad's register book as "Jonathan Gibson, of Springfield, Illinois." He wrote in very large, very fancy Spencerian handwriting and took up three whole lines in my book. Yes, he had escorted her to the hotel, carrying her valise and carpetbag. All I could remember about his behavior in the Nomad was that Jonah had said that he didn't eat much of his salt pork at dinner and only half of his beans.

"Do you know him, Aunt Lily?"

She nodded. "Yes, he's a nice man. He sat in the seat across from me on the train."

"What's he doing out here?"

"Taking photographs."

"He's a photographer?"

"Yes." She showed a dimple in one cheek when she smiled. Then she giggled again.

Photographer? I thought of Aunt Willa's wanting a portrait of Mr. Ponder. "Aunt Lily, did Mr. Gibson bring his camera with him?"

"Well, of course, Damaris. A person can't make photographs of the scenery and the Indians without a camera and all the other things he needs. Didn't you notice the big black case he had? It has his camera and plates and chemicals in it."

"I saw it, but I didn't know what was in it. Do you think he'd take pictures of some of us if we paid him to?"

"Oh, I'm sure he would. He takes photographs of people all the time. He says that's how he gets enough money to take pictures of mountains and rivers, the things he really wants to photograph."

"Good. I know a lady who wants a photograph of Mr. Ponder."

"How strange! Well, I'm sure Jonathan would oblige her if Mr. Ponder will sit for him. Jonathan has already asked to take some portraits of me."

Jonathan? I eyed Aunt Lily out of the corner of one eye.

All at once she asked me, "What's the weather like here in the spring and summer?" I wondered about that question, too. It seemed to me like a fast change of subject from Jonathan.

I told her, "Terrible. Mostly hot! It doesn't rain at all from April to June, but we have some good stormy, rainy weather in July and August. The rest of the year we don't have good weather either. We have dust storms, so it's dry all over again."

She said softly, "It's no wonder your mother looks poorly—with all this work to do, your father gone, and this climate."

I nodded. It was cool now because it wasn't April yet, and the kitchen was comfortable even with the stove going full blast and the laundry boiling in copper tubs on its top. How I hated that constant laundry! It had no mercy at all.

I said, "I'm surely glad you're here, Aunt Lily. You can take some of the work load off Mama."

"Well, I'll try to, Damaris. I can't say I really liked the sign I saw at your desk, though."

I understood. I had hand lettered, "No gun fighting in here, please. Settle your troubles with fists, rocks, or bricks, if you can find one, outside."

My sign had made a lot of tough-looking men laugh and talk to each other about it. We hadn't had any real trouble at all.

Aunt Lily said again, "We'll see how it goes, Damaris."

It went pretty well for a whole month. Mr. Gibson stayed much longer than I had expected him to. He made photographs of all of us but mostly of Arthur and Mahkto, because they were the most interesting, I supposed. He had a couple of cameras, a little camera around his neck that he used to catch people unawares. I didn't like it. It worked very fast, making a clicking sound, which was the only warning you had.

The bigger camera, a Tourograph, which stood on three legs, took longer to take pictures, and it was no fun sitting for your portrait when he used it. He used what he called gelatin dry plates with it, and he developed them out in Brown Betty's wickiup, the darkest place around, in tubs he bought from Mr. Baynor. Mr. Gibson's fingers were always stained because of the developer he used, and he smelled to high heaven of chemicals all the time.

Even though he was an "artist" according to Aunt Lily, I thought Mr. Gibson was a painful person. He complained that William's and Ann Viola's freckles made them come out badly in photographs, as if they had the measles. I hated the mirrors he used to reflect light on me as I sat inside on a lobby chair, trying not to breathe while he took my photograph. When I'd fidget, he'd tell me, "You moved!" Or, "Confound it, you breathed too deeply. Stop breathing." At least, he didn't take portraits with those uncomfortable head clamps that had been used on me in Saint Louis when I was a child.

Mostly Mr. Gibson took pictures of Aunt Lily. He posed her from the back, smiling over her shoulder at him. He photographed her from the front sitting on the sofa in her best gown trying to stifle giggles and not breathe while holding a velvet rose taken off her fanciest hat. He posed her against a background of a big cactus, a mountain in the distance, by sunset, by dawn's early light, and up in Mr. Ponder's wagon pretending to drive the team. He must have used up plate after plate on her, and then he'd send off to San Diego for more plates.

Mr. Ponder didn't have to tell me what was going on, but he did anyhow one afternoon in the first week of March during a dust storm. "That photographer jasper is pretty smitten with your charming auntie, ain't he?"

"So it appears, Mr. Ponder." I was adding up a column of numbers.

"And she seems to dote on him, don't she?"

"Some people might say that she did."

At the moment Mr. Gibson was with Mama and Aunt Lily, taking pictures of them making beds. I doubted if a photograph of two ladies, who looked a lot alike, making a bed in a hotel room would interest anyone very much unless the picture gave a good view of how the Nomad was constructed. After all, I knew enough now to realize that there were very few hotels like mine anywhere in the United States. By crumbs, it could easily be the only one!

Next Mr. Ponder wanted to know, "Have you heard anything from your Aunt Willa about that likeness of me you sent her?"

"Nary a word."

"What do you suppose she had in mind when she asked for it?" He never gave up.

I shut the accounts book and told him, "Mr. Ponder, people keep telling me that I'm like my Aunt Willa in some ways, but that doesn't mean I know what goes on in her head a thousand miles away." I could catch Mama's thoughts at times, but I had never truly been able to do that with Aunt Willa.

He shook his head. I smelled bay rum on him as

he said, "Your Aunt Willa don't do things jest because she takes an idle notion to. Wanting that picture of yours truly has a meaning."

"I don't think she means to give it to a sheriff to put out as a wanted poster." In a way I felt sorry for Mr. Ponder, but all the same I wanted to laugh at him.

He only gave me another shake of his head. "You're a hardy little trout, ain't you?"

I supposed that was another way of saying a "terror on two feet."

I stuffed the accounts book into my apron pocket and went to find Mama and Aunt Lily. There wasn't any point in my getting peeved with Mr. Ponder. It wasn't worth it. We were doing well at the Nomad. All was going along smooth as satin.

And then on the fifteenth of March, "the dangerous Ides of March," according to Mr. Wroth, my world and Mama's fell apart at the seams again.

We got up that morning to find Aunt Lily and Mr. Gibson sitting side by side on my red sofa, holding hands. She was all dressed up in her crystal blue silk dress. The velvet rose was back on top of her pansy-covered best hat. The photographer was dressed in the black slouch hat he came to town in and the black frock coat he wore when he took photographs of grown-ups who would pay him. Aunt Lily's carpetbag and valise and his bag and big black case were piled at their feet.

"Lucy!" Aunt Lily and Mr. Gibson got up together when they spotted Mama and me. My aunt was blushing pink as a carnation. She giggled, then started chattering right away in a high voice. What she said chilled my spine, though. "Mr. Gibson asked me to marry him last night!"

"Yes, Mrs. Boyd." Gibson had a bass voice. "There's an eight o'clock train to Leacock. We're going down there to find a preacher."

"I hope you will both be very happy." Mama's words had a hollow sound to me.

I didn't wish them well. I was losing a chambermaid and laundry worker. "Aunt Lily, are you coming back here then?" I asked.

"No, Damaris." She wasn't looking at me at all. She was looking at Mr. Gibson. Bosh, I'd been kerflummoxed again.

He was still looking at her when he told us, "From Leacock we're going to San Diego, so I can take photographs of the old Spanish missions up and down California."

"We don't want a wedding present," my aunt added.

I was tempted to say that people who eloped didn't deserve wedding gifts. She was silly. I'd liked her being like a kid back in Massachusetts last year, but not out here. She was too old for that. People grew up fast in Arizona Territory! I said, "I'm glad, Aunt Lily, that you are happy now." Mama had told me

she'd been jilted three times back in the East. I figured that the three men had got so tired of her silly
ways they'd run away from her. No wonder she was
eloping. She'd learned one thing out of three failures.
She most likely didn't want to give Mr. Gibson time
to reconsider. That's why she was being so hasty now.

I didn't escort the happy pair to the train. I stomped
over to Mr. Baynor's, dodging windblown tumble-
weeds on the way. From there I sent a telegram to
Aunt Willa. It said:

No news from Papa yet. Aunt Lily has eloped
with a man she met here. It is not Mr. Ponder.
Please quit your job and come back to help or
send us someone to help. Send a good worker.

Love,
Damaris Boyd

In a way I'd miss Aunt Lily. Because she was a
farmer's daughter she had had a real way with our
cow—better than William. Mama had lived in Saint
Louis too long to please Brown Betty.

All the same Aunt Lily's giddiness and the romances she brought in one of her bags and read over
and over again had worn on me. I'd looked at the
titles: *A Desperate Deed, The Broken Betrothal,
Haunted Hearts,* and one called *Motherless.* They
were as bad as Jess King's dime novels, though I had
to admit Aunt Lily's books cost only a nickel.

I surely hoped that Aunt Willa would ship somebody out to Switzer Wells fast to help us with the
laundry. I had Arthur and Mahkto carry signs alongside the trains coming and going, but they hadn't
done us one bit of good.

Sometimes Chinese men ran laundries in other
places in the West. I hoped that one or two would
come to town and set up in business either for himself or in our place. Mr. Toy would be happy to have
somebody to talk with.

11

MORE THAN ENOUGH

Five days later Mr. Baynor caught William on his way out of his store coming home from school and gave him the telegram Aunt Willa had just sent me over the wires. It was short. She didn't waste words, not when you had to pay for each one. All it said was:

Mrs. Dooley is on her way.

Fondly,
Willa Boyd

I had to hunt for Mama to show it her. She'd been running around all morning setting ant traps. Ants had come into the lobby and kitchen the night before in a parade an inch wide. We'd swept them out, but that didn't stop them. They were very determined insects. She and Arthur had put wrung-out sponges sprinkled with sugar on plates all around the Nomad before noon. Now the sponges were full of ants, and she was going from plate to plate picking up the sponges and dumping them into the bucket of boiling water Arthur carried.

It had been a bad day in other ways too. Ann Viola was in bed with a sore throat, eating onions that had been boiled in molasses. Cousin Jonah had had the hiccups so badly that he couldn't wait on guests at noon and had to keep taking teaspoonfuls of vinegar to stop them. I'd served lunch. My feet ached, and I worried about matters in the future more than I let on.

Mostly Mama worried me. I'd seen the big bottle of tincture of lavender in her room and the teaspoon beside it. She'd taken that sometimes for faintness back home, but she'd never kept it beside her bed before. She'd taken Aunt Lily's running off pretty hard.

To comfort her, I showed her Aunt Willa's telegram and asked her, "Who's Mrs. Dooley?"

"I have no idea, Damaris. I've never heard of such a person." Mama was cross, as Arthur and I followed her to another plate and sponge of ants. "I presume Mrs. Dooley is some woman who's to work here. I pray to heaven she'll stay long enough for us to get to know her."

I agreed. "Shall I tell Mr. Ponder she's coming?" I asked.

Arthur answered, surprising me, "No, he don't care about the married ones, Rising Moon."

I agreed with Arthur too. It was *Mrs.* Dooley. My hopes rose. Perhaps Mr. Dooley would come with her. There wasn't a place for him at the Nomad, but with Switzer Wells booming the way it was, he could find work just about anywhere. That might keep Mrs. Dooley working for me.

So Mama and I waited for her to arrive, hoping that she was a good washer and ironer. Because she was coming from civilized Saint Louis, we didn't even consider her as a milker.

On the third day after I'd received Aunt Willa's telegram, we heard from Mrs. Dooley. It was another telegram. It had been sent from Leacock and said:

Miss Damaris Boyd. I missed the train to Switzer Wells. Can somebody come in a wagon and get me?

Belinda Dooley

I was a little bit put out by anybody missing a train. Mrs. Dooley could wait a couple of days in Leacock for the next one, but maybe she didn't have the money for a hotel there. And, by crumbs, we needed her now!

So I went to Mr. Ponder and asked him to take the wagon down to Leacock and bring her back with him. He wasn't doing anything else around the Nomad of any consequence. I was careful to tell him that she was a Mrs., not a Miss, which should warn him not to make a fool of himself again.

He didn't come back when we expected him. But then he seldom did. I guessed he'd gone to visit the Last Chance Saloon in Leacock, an old haunt of his. I was sure he was making the most of his liberty, away from us at the Nomad, though he only sat around in the lobby. I figured he'd put Mrs. Dooley up in a hotel there while he "painted Leacock pink."

Finally he did show up, though, traveling by daylight because the weather was cooler now. There was a plumpish woman sitting beside him on the driver's seat of the wagon. As a matter of fact, she was driving Victor and Treasureen. He was lolling back, smoking a cheroot. She was dressed all in black, very dusty black. Mrs. Dooley was a widow! Well, that meant no Mr. Dooley.

I went out to the wagon to greet her and said, "I'm Damaris Boyd. You must be Mrs. Dooley."

She didn't say a word. She only gave the reins to Mr. Ponder, who did the talking. He grinned at me and said, "No, little lady, you got it wrong this time." Oh, he was very pleased with himself! "She used to be Mrs. Dooley. Now she's Mrs. Malachi Ponder. She takes a man like a bramble off a briar, she does. She's my bride. We tied the knot yesterday morning in Leacock."

My jaw fell onto my chest. I couldn't do anything but shake my head at the two of them.

The new Mrs. Ponder, who had to be his age and not one bit handsome either, got down out of the wagon by herself, huffing and puffing. She took my hand and shook it, then said in a husky voice, "That aunt 'a yers is a wonder-worker of a woman. I never did think a old maid like her could deliver the goods fer me so fast."

"Deliver the goods?" I asked her.

"Sure. When I signed up and paid her the twenty dollars at her Lonely Hearts Bureau, she came up right off with dear Malachi's picture. Because I said I liked what I saw, she sent me out here fast."

Lonely Hearts Bureau? By the seven sleeping sisters, Aunt Willa had said that she had gone into business! She was running a marriage bureau.

I said, "But Aunt Willa sent me a telegram saying you'd come out here to work for us."

"Oh, dearie, that was my second choice in case dear Malachi and I didn't hit it off. Your aunt said the woods out here is full of bachelors lookin' for wives."

I stared at Mr. Ponder. "What about somebody to do our laundry?" I asked. As far as I was concerned, he was a robber. I wanted his bride to know that I thought so.

As for her, I'd bet anything she missed the train on purpose, knowing he would be sent after her in the only wagon the Nomad had. Belinda Ponder struck me as a woman who knew her oats.

I knew mine, too, but I wasn't sneaky about it. I

told her, "Oh, come on in and meet my mother and cousin."

"I won't stay but a couple of minutes," the new Mrs. Ponder informed me. "And then dear Malachi and I'll be on our way. We only come up here to get his duds and then we're off to Saint Louis for a honeymoon, so's I can show him off to my relations." She folded her arms, sending up a cloud of road dust. Her forceful way made me sigh. She was a strong-looking woman with muscles, dyed black hair, and little, round blue eyes. She had the look of a good laundry worker. While I was feeling sorry for Mama and myself, Mrs. Ponder kept on talking. "We won't be comin' back here, so I might as well tell you right out that Malachi don't want to be yer partner in this big tent no more." She stared at the Nomad and sniffed. I couldn't tell if it was because of dust or disgust.

"He doesn't want to be my partner anymore!" I didn't even try to keep the pleasure out of my voice. By crumbs, this cloud had a silver lining all right. At last the Nomad was going to be mine alone!

Mrs. Ponder went on, "No, dear Malachi don't. He wants you to buy him out of the partnership."

"Come in and meet my mother," I repeated. I stepped aside, so she could go into the lobby. When she was out of sight, I went up to the wagon and said to Mr. Ponder, who was looking down the street of Switzer Wells as if he was saying farewell forever to it, "Mr. Ponder, please look me in the eye and tell me the truth. Did you want to help run this hotel or did you become partners with Aunt Willa and me so you could court her?"

He said, removing the cheroot from his mouth, "The hotel business holds no charms for me. I am more at home in a livery stable."

So it was as I had thought. "How much money do you want to sell yourself out of the partnership?" I asked him. I knew he had heard what his wife had said.

"Two hundred dollars'll do the trick. That's twice as much as I put in. That's enough profit for me."

I nodded, put up my hand, and we shook on the bargain. It seemed a fair enough deal to me, too. "Mr. Ponder, what about the wagon and the team?"

"I plan to sell Victor and Treasureen and the wagon down in Leacock."

That's what I had figured. "I'll go get Mahkto to watch the team and ask Arthur to help you pack your things," I said. Then I wanted to know, "What about Arthur? Will you be taking him to Missouri with you?" I had it in mind to embarrass Mr. Ponder by letting him know that I thought he was deserting his Apache friend for a lady he scarcely knew.

He was ready for my question, though. That was one of the big troubles with grown-ups. They thought ahead a lot of the time, and when you thought you had them, they fired back at you. "No, little lady, Saint Louis is no place for a Apache to settle down and be happy. I think Arthur'll stay here with you rather than traipse off with me. And I don't think Belinda would take to him in any event."

I was sure of that. I doubted if Arthur would take to her either. I certainly hadn't.

After I'd written up an agreement breaking our partnership and had Mr. Baynor witness Mr. Ponder's signing of it, I gave Ponder two hundred dollars in gold out of my mattress. He and Belinda stayed to supper but not overnight, probably because the Nomad wasn't elegant enough for honeymooners in her estimation. She really thought he was a catch! I didn't understand it. If he'd been what I'd caught, I would have thrown him back into the water. It was a sight to watch her lallygagging over him all through dinner. I was happy to see the Ponders drive off at dusk for Leacock.

But even if my hotel was now entirely mine, I had problems. We still didn't have anybody to help with the laundry. I'd have to keep looking for someone, and Arthur and Mahkto would have to meet every train that came through with the signs.

A week went by and nobody got off the train to help us. Nobody in Switzer Wells wanted to wash dirty clothes and towels and tablecloths for anybody but themselves, it seemed. I sent Ann Viola and

William door to door throughout the town asking for hired help, but no one came to the Nomad.

I tried to aid Mama as best I could, but now because I was the desk clerk and the manager and accounts keeper, I couldn't do very much. And nobody else around the hotel was willing to help with the laundry! Arthur and Mahkto let me know without saying a word how they felt about doing laundry. They just walked away when I mentioned it to them.

Finally I had a talk with Mr. Wroth out in the lobby about my troubles. Mama had finished one bottle of tincture of lavender and bought another and was dosing herself with it. It was disappearing fast too. That told me, as Mama wouldn't, that she was having a lot of faint spells.

The teacher understood. He didn't ever say much around the place, but he had eyes in his head. He'd seen how matters had been with Aunt Willa, Aunt Lily, and Mr. and Mrs. Ponder.

As he leaned back in his chair after setting up the chessboard ready for his and Jonah's game that night, he told me, "You know, Damaris, what you need around here is a man who'll take hold of things. A man who'll give his whole time to the running of this hotel."

My hopes rose. Was he going to offer himself and quit teaching school? Teachers were easier to get than laundry workers!

No, he wasn't. My hopes fell. He said what I'd been thinking all along, "You need your father here, Damaris."

"Yes, sir." Papa was just what we needed. "But we don't even know for sure where he is," I said.

"Damaris, I suspect he is still at the goldfields. If he'd gone back to Missouri, some member of your family would surely have told him where you are now that your Aunt Willa has returned there. Surely he would have telegraphed you or come out here to bring you back home with him."

True, all too true. I sighed.

"He seems to be a rather strange man to me." Mr. Wroth was looking at a chess piece, not at me.

I wasn't about to fly off the handle at him for criticizing Papa. "Papa has a disease," I said. "It's called get-rich-quick. It runs in the Boyd family."

Mr. Wroth chuckled. "A lot of men have that disease. It doesn't strike teachers, or they wouldn't be teachers." Then he asked, "Why don't you send somebody to bring your father back here? Get him here before your mother collapses of overwork."

So he had noticed that too. Yes sir, Mr. Wroth had helped over the weekends with the laundry. He was nice.

Cousin Jonah came over and sat down across from the teacher. It was time for the chess match.

I said, "Thank you, Mr. Wroth." Then I went back to the room I was alone in now that Aunt Willa and Aunt Lily had gone. On the way I looked into Mama's room. It was only nine thirty, but she was in bed. She'd gone to bed right after she'd got the laundry on the line.

I sat down on my bed and consulted the *Ladies' Indispensable Assistant,* but this time it failed to tell me what to do. Finally, to comfort myself, I counted the coins in my mattress that made for restless nights because the old mattress was very thin and the money clattered when I rolled over. But this time the money didn't comfort me.

I considered matters carefully and came to a conclusion. Arizona Territory was Indian country, so it would be wise of me to consult an Indian.

I found Arthur squatting on the ground out behind the hotel enjoying the stars, I supposed, talking to Mahkto in Apache. He finished what he was saying, looked up at me, and asked, "You need me, Rising Moon?"

"Well, I might at that." I got the milking stool out of Brown Betty's wickiup, brought it over, and sat down. Then I told Arthur what Mr. Wroth had said. I finished with, "Will you carry a letter from me to Papa?"

Arthur didn't say anything for a time. Then finally he said, "I don't know that country east of here. Send Mahkto. He's been there with his band." He spoke softly to Mahkto in Apache.

Mahkto nodded.

Arthur told me, "He says he'll take you anywhere you want to go."

Me? Me go out into the wilds with Mahkto? He wasn't only an Apache Indian; he was younger than I was.

"Mahkto will take care of you, Rising Moon."

I told Arthur, "But we don't have a wagon or any horses."

"You don't need a wagon," said Arthur. "Get yourself some horses and go."

"No, my mother would never let me." Instead I suggested, "Maybe I could send Cousin Jonah or ask Uncle Owen to go."

Arthur shook his head. "Not them. Mahkto won't go if they go."

"Well, why not?"

"They boss him around. He don't like it. He's the son of a chief."

I stared at Mahkto, who was looking at the moon, which had just climbed over the eastern mountains. He didn't look much like a chief's son to me. "What's he doing here at my hotel if he's that important, Arthur?"

"The chief sent him to his mother's band before his father's people went down to Old Mexico to get away from the soldiers. The chief wanted Mahkto to know the white man's ways."

Aha! Mahkto's band were hostile Indians fighting the U.S. Army. Mahkto was an Indian spy. So that was why he had talked with Cuchillo, who, according to Mr. Baynor, had been a "bad actor" a number of years ago, though he was "peaceable enough" now.

I asked Arthur sourly, "Well, what does Mahkto think of white men after he's lived with us?"

"He thinks white men are queer and have queer ways."

I said, "You know, Arthur, I wouldn't go across the street alone with Mahkto. I think some Apache ways are very queer."

Arthur said, "Take somebody with you when you go."

I told him, "I can't spare anybody here." Jonah was my best bet to go, of course, but if Mahkto didn't take to him, what could I do about it? And besides I had to have somebody to wait on the tables.

Suddenly Arthur put in, "Don't take anybody out of here, Rising Moon. Take somebody useless."

"Mr. Ponder's gone, Arthur." How right that station agent at Leacock had been about Ponder!

Arthur told me softly, "Jess King is here."

"Her? Railroad Rob?"

"Her pa's got horses."

By crumbs, Mr. King did have. Three of them. Sometimes he went into the desert prospecting for a couple of days himself. I guessed the hotel business didn't truly charm him. To tell the truth, it didn't charm me either a good deal of the time. It certainly wasn't a soft snap working seven days a week.

"Arthur, ask Mahkto, please, how long it would take to get to where he thinks Papa might be and bring him back?" I had no idea if Mahkto knew where Papa was, but this seemed to me to be the easiest way to put the question.

By the powders of war—to borrow a saying from Mr. Ponder—Mahkto seemed to think he knew! I saw him hold up both hands, his ten fingers spread, after Arthur had talked to him. Ten days! Mahkto grinned at me, the first smile I had ever had from him. He wanted to go!

I was so kerflummoxed at the thought that I got up, and after I said thank you to Arthur, I went straight to bed. I couldn't sleep, though, for thinking. If there is any one thing that stops sleep, it has to be thinking.

The next afternoon, after school, I went over to the Casa del Rey to see little old Jess. She was lying on her stomach on her bed reading a new dime novel about detectives, not railroaders this time.

"May I sit down?" I asked her. I figured that would catch her off guard. I had never called on her before.

"Rest your feet, kid," she told me.

So I sat on her bed. I came straight to the point. "Jess, I'm going on an adventure. I need your secrecy and your help."

"What's up, kid?" I could see that the dime-novel detectives were a rough-talking lot. Jess sat up.

I told her about my talks with Mr. Wroth and Arthur. Like everybody else in Switzer Wells, she knew all about our troubles with my aunts and Mr. Ponder. "Jess, I am going out with Mahkto to find my father. I need to rent two horses. I don't dare ask any of the grown-ups around here for them. They'd stop me from going for sure."

"Dead in your tracks," she agreed. "When are you going?"

"Tomorrow night at midnight." I figured that was a good time.

"A dark and ghastly hour, pardner," said Jess, who muddled up her language something terrible at times.

"Partner?"

She stuck out her hand. "You can rent horses and horse gear from me only on one condition. You have to take me along with you. I'll even throw in our pack burro for free if you do."

Even though Arthur had already suggested that she come, I hesitated. "Your father will have a fit. Your mother will too."

"Well, what about your mother?"

"Now look here, Jess. My mother's got Ann Viola and William. You're an only child."

"That's true. It does make me more valuable, doesn't it?" That seemed to please her, as I thought it might. "I'll leave a letter for Pa saying I've gone away," she said. "You know, I've been out to the desert with him a couple of times. He'll know I can take care of myself. I know what supplies he takes when he goes out prospecting. I'll get everything ready for us." She smiled at me and said as if she recited, "All will be in readiness at midnight at the edge of town." Then she smiled. "You only have to bring your duds and that Apache of yours."

Everything was happening far too fast for me. "Jess, why do you want to go too? You don't have to." I was wary. What was her game now? I'd been through too many of them already.

"To get out of school for ten days, I'll do just about anything, pardner. Mr. Wroth is going to give us two arithmetic tests next week."

Clearly this wasn't a game for her. I shook my head at her and said, "Shame on you." Then I shook her hand, which was still sticking out.

Just before I left and she went back to her dime novel, she asked me two things, "Do you trust that Apache not to deliver us up to savage Indians in the wilds?"

"I think so. His father's band's gone to Old Mexico." I did trust Mahkto.

She looked doubtful but asked me, "Can you steal a pair of your brother's britches? My pa doesn't have any sidesaddles."

"Yes, I can get them off the clothesline tomorrow night."

"Good. *Vaya con Dios,* pardner, until our fateful

rendezvous tomorrow night." That was a dime-novel sentence if I had ever heard one.

"Vaya con Dios," I told her. And I left. I knew that those Spanish words meant "Go with God." I planned to do some praying tonight and even more during the next ten days. It wasn't only that I was worried about tracking down Papa's whereabouts. I was worried about how Mama would take to my leaving home in the middle of the night.

I would never have admitted it six months ago, but it seemed to me that Jess King and I were thinking alike these days. Either that or I had rubbed off on her since the night of the thunder and lightning storm when I told her what I thought of her. Or she was rubbing off on me. I planned to leave a letter for Mama as she did for her father. I'd already made it up in my head. It would say:

> I've gone off with Jess King to bring Papa home from the diggings wherever they are. Don't worry about us. We are in good hands. Mahkto is our guide. Tell Cousin Jonah to be the desk clerk and the waiter and manager. Rely on Arthur for everything else. Make Ann Viola sleep on my mattress at night to keep everything safe there.
>
> Love from your daughter,
> Damaris

I'd write it and shove it under her door just before midnight. By the time Mama found it in the morning, the three of us would be miles away from Switzer Wells.

William's britches were his first long ones, Levis recently bought at Mr. Baynor's. I felt guilty taking them off the clothesline because of that. He was so proud of them. But he'd understand after he saw the letter I'd left. The Levis were damp but fit me all right. As I walked through Switzer Wells to the rendezvous at the north end of town in them, I decided that pants were a real improvement over skirts.

Mahkto had gone to the rendezvous earlier to inspect what Jess had got ready for the journey. Equipment had to be just right before anyone went out into the desert.

I found Mahkto at the edge of town, mounted on a horse that shone silvery gray in the moonlight. Little old Jess was standing beside a sorrel I'd seen her riding before. There was a little black horse for me, saddled, bridled, and ready to go. Jess was holding its reins, and she also held onto the lead rope of a burro.

She whispered to me, "That Apache of yours looked at what was on the burro and said 'Okay.' I guess he meant we have enough water and food."

That was good. *Okay* was a word Mahkto had learned sometime back from William. It was a word Mama despised.

Jess went on whispering, "Reach into my belt and take one of them."

"All right." I had no idea what she meant, but it would be wise to humor her, so I felt around her waist under her belt. My Lord, there were two pistols there, one on each side of the buckle!

"Put one of them in your belt and see to it that that Apache of yours is always riding up ahead of us."

I didn't have a belt, but William's Levis were tight around the waist, so I put the pistol inside them, jabbing myself in the lower rib. I whispered back to her, "Jess, that's where guides always are, up in front."

"And that's where he's going to stay, pardner. I'll have my eagle eye on him by night while you keep yours on him by day. Now mount up on Sable Satan."

I couldn't say the horse's name surprised me. I only hoped he didn't feel he had to live up to it.

Then Jess asked, "Are you sure that Apache knows where he's going?"

"I think he does."

I'd talked to Arthur about that, and he'd talked a long time to Mahkto. Mahkto had come to Boyd Valley just before we'd made our one and only visit there. Mahkto claimed that from where he and some other Apaches of his father's band were, up in the mountains, they'd seen white men working in a valley below. He'd seen miners before. That's what these men were. And these miners were located in the right direction for Papa to be. I surely hoped that Mahkto was right. It would be terrible if we went to a gold camp that Papa wasn't in. We had to trust to luck— and to Mahkto.

He led us as though he knew where he was going all right. And my horse trusted him, or he trusted Mahkto's gray. I didn't know which. My animal walked right behind his while I hung on to the saddle horn. I wasn't a horseback rider but a carriage rider. After the first hour of riding I was ready to fall off Sable Satan and rest, but Mahkto went right on going and Jess was behind me, pulling the burro along.

Miles out of Switzer Wells Mahkto astonished me by starting to sing. I couldn't believe what the song was. The piece William had sung in a music recital in Saint Louis, "I'm the Governor's Only Son." Mahkto wasn't exactly tuneful, but his singing told me that he was in good spirits, which should mean that he knew where he was going.

I was afraid that we'd be trailed by someone Mama sent out, but luck was with us. It was probably because of the dust storm that we were saved. Because it was nearly April and getting hot in the daytime, Mahkto stopped around noon. Jess put up a canvas shelter for her and me just before the dust hit us. We'd seen it coming out of the south like a dark wall over the desert and sky. Any hoof marks our animals left would be covered by the blowing sand and dirt.

Mahkto wouldn't come into our tent. He tethered

the horses and burro to some little trees I didn't know the names of and rolled up in one of Jess's blankets under a creosote bush. Perhaps he slept, but Jess and I surely didn't, not only because of the noisy storm and gritty wind that blew in on us under our blankets but because we were scared. The desert could give anyone the willies and make her say her prayers.

When the dust had passed, Mahkto wouldn't let us build a fire. I guessed it was because the smoke might be seen. So the three of us ate dried biscuits, some dried meat that tasted like string, and drank water from our canteens. The sight of our pistols didn't seem to faze our Apache one bit. He looked at them and then looked away.

I was so sore that night that Jess had to shove me on my horse before we could start out again. Her gentleness made me forgive her everything. I remembered a sentence from a book I'd read in the sixth grade and said, "You are one of nature's noblemen, Jess King."

She beamed. I could see her teeth flash in the moonlight with joy. The rest of that night she rode beside me telling me that we'd better watch out for rattlesnakes when we camped in the morning to get out of the sun.

We traveled north by east all the time. By moonlight the desert was mysterious, all silver and black and ghostlike. By day it was gray-brown; gray-brown rocks, dried-out grass, powdery dirt, and dusty bushes.

Later, according to Jess, it could be pretty, covered with wild flowers that didn't last more than a couple of days. But it wasn't pretty now.

Wonder of wonders, one night we saw a camel off in the distance, or at least what I thought looked like one. It was very large and stood under the stars not taking any notice of us at all. I could scarcely believe my eyes and called out to Jess, who said she saw it, too, and thought we'd better speed up and get away from it. Horses hated camels. They gave a horse the willies in the worst way and made them run away and rear.

Of course, we saw other animals and birds too, lots of them, but mostly jackrabbits. Once at dawn I saw a good-sized desert tortoise crawling along. It seemed to me to be going as fast as we were, and that wasn't fast enough. We were heading for mountains that didn't seem to get one bit nearer as we covered the miles.

On the second day Mahkto made a fire for us himself, a little one but big enough to boil some canned corned beef in a skillet with onions and water. It tasted just fine. The day after that Jess shot two quail, and we roasted them over another fire. She could shoot and she could cook. I began truly to respect her. The rest of the time we lived on dried biscuits. By the time we'd reached the mountains I was tired of biscuits and warm water. Bread and water was all right for prisoners, but not for travelers.

We didn't know the names of the mountains, though I supposed Mahkto had an Apache name for them. They were peaks of red rock and, in a way, pretty. But I was tired of seeing rocks. What I liked about the mountains were the trees, green ones, pines and junipers smelling sweet as perfume.

Our mountain camp was beside a stream so filled with trout that we caught some with our bare hands. That night Jess and I ate fried fish but, of course, not Mahkto. He caught a fat wood rat in a trap he made and boiled it in a tin can for his meal. We didn't watch him eat, and he didn't watch us. It worked out just fine, and after we'd eaten we sat together around the fire when a cougar started screaming in the night.

I had no idea where we were, and I worried and prayed but without telling Jess. I worried, too, about how Mama was taking my leaving. It wasn't truly as if I was running away. I'd said where I was going, the people I was going with, why I was going, and that I'd be back. I hoped she would understand. I was doing it for her sake, not for mine. Horseback travel wasn't my idea of the way to get about. I was saddle-sore, and I wasn't at all sure that Jess's black horse liked me. He lived up to his name in some ways. He'd tried to twist his head around and bite the stirrup with my foot in it twice while we were winding our way down out of the mountains on what only an Apache could call a trail.

Yet Mahkto never seemed lost. Sometimes he'd rein

in the gray and look around him for a while. Then he'd start right off again.

Early in the morning of the fifth day Mahkto stopped suddenly ahead of me in a stand of scrubby little pines. We'd been descending all night. Because I was half asleep, my horse's nose almost bumped into the tail of his gray. I knew that Sable Satan had hopes of biting the gray too, so I pulled his head up just in time.

Mahkto turned in his saddle and said with a grin, "Okay." And then he pointed.

I looked where he pointed. Down below us less than a mile away was a wide green valley with a river winding through it. There were a couple of log houses there on the riverbank and something else—more tents than I'd ever seen before in my life. It was a gold camp. I was pretty sure of that, but was it the camp Papa and Mr. Benjamin had gone to?

Well, there was only one way to find out. I nudged Sable Satan with my heels out ahead of Mahkto's horse and started down the hillside. From now on, I would be doing the leading.

As I went past Mahkto I nodded at him and said, "Thank you."

"Okay," came from him again. He knew what I meant, though.

12

SHOWDOWN!

Jess caught up with me as we came out onto the floor
of the valley. She said, "You've sure got a way with
that Apache of yours. Never once did he play you
false. I had my eagle eye on him constantly."

"Mahkto's our friend." I still had no idea how
much English Mahkto understood, but I said it very
loudly so he could hear the compliment. There was
no telling what went on in an Apache's mind, but the
words might please him. He'd earned them. I doubted
if he would understand the fancy dime-novel language Jess used, but I wasn't even sure about that.
As Mr. Ponder had once told me, Apaches weren't
one bit dumb. Maybe Mahkto didn't read books yet,
but he knew about a lot of other things. I was sure
that he had learned a great deal about the "white
man's ways" by now. Living at my crazy hotel ought
to educate anyone. I just hoped Mahkto didn't get all

of his ideas of white people from the way we lived at the Nomad and from Uncle Owen.

I said to Jess, "I forgive you for all of those lizards, Jess. Are you going to be thrashed by your father when you get back home?"

"More than likely, thrashed by both of them. My stepmother will take up a stick. Pa, he does it by hand."

This wasn't good news. I said, "Jess, tell your father that I'll pay for the use of the horses and everything else."

"I was going to already. Will you be whipped, Damaris?"

"Maybe. Maybe by Mama when I get home, though I'm as big as she is now." I sighed. "And I might get a whipping right here today from Papa, if he's here."

Jess said, "You're brave, Damaris. That could happen pretty soon, couldn't it?"

What she said made me want to laugh. Brave? I was scared, more scared now than I'd been in the desert and the mountains. I'd been brave for a long time it seemed to me. If my father was truly here, I might not be able to keep it up.

No, deep down I wasn't really that much like Aunt Willa, though I had some of her traits. And, too, deep down, I wasn't all that taken with the idea of being a hotelkeeper. It was a terrible responsibility. Maybe after a time I'd get to be like Aunt Willa in other ways, but I hadn't got to it yet. I didn't have her confidence in herself. I hadn't seen Papa in ten months. It wasn't easy being a business lady, though I had to admit that it was worth it most of the time.

The first people we came across were two men beside the shallow river. They were shoveling dirt from the banks into a long wooden contraption that I learned later trapped flecks of gold in cleated boxes when water was poured over the dirt. Both of them wore pistols, I noticed. One of them reached for a rifle propped up against a tree.

"Hey," I called out, "don't shoot us. We're looking for someone. We're from Switzer Wells."

Jess told me in a hurry, "They think we're going to jump their claim because we're strangers."

"What does that mean, Jess?"

"That we'll drive them away from their flume and say the land is ours, or we'll take their gold out of the flume."

So that was what get-rich-quick drove people to! No wonder the disease had such a bad reputation. I called out again, "The Indian's a friend of ours. I'm Damaris Boyd." I jerked my head toward Jess. "This is Jessica King."

Jess didn't snort in disgust or say, "No, I'm Jess." This was a better place to be a Jessica than a Jess, and no place at all to claim to be Jesse James.

"Gals? Little gals, way out here?" The man who'd

grabbed the rifle lowered it and stared popeyed at us.

The other miner took off his hat and asked, "What can we do for you ladies?"

I rode straight up to them, reined in, and said, "I'm looking for my father. His name is Charles Boyd. Is he here?"

The first miner looked at the other one. Then he said, "Do you know anybody named Boyd?"

"Nope, but I don't know every man in these diggings by a long shot neither. I tell you what, ladies, you ask over at the assay office. It's over there, the biggest cabin." He leaned on his shovel and pointed.

I said, "Thank you," and the three of us rode on our way. Everybody stared at us as we went by, but no one threatened us. I suppose it wasn't every day two girls and an Apache Indian came riding together into camp. The miners surely gawked at us.

The assay office was a little place partitioned off in the back by iron bars. A man was sitting in that cage at a desk. There was a scale in front of him. Later I learned it was for weighing gold dust and nuggets miners brought in. The cage was to keep the miners out, not the assayer in.

The assayer looked up surprised to see Jess and me, two girls with their long hair in pigtails. He asked, "What are you girls doing here?"

I said, "Looking for my father, sir. His name is Charles Boyd, and he's from Saint Louis, Missouri."

The assayer shook his head. "That name doesn't

come to mind. Sorry. There's lots of men hereabouts."

Despair grabbed me. It looked to me as if Mahkto had led us to the wrong camp. And then, by crumbs, I thought of something else. "Mister, do you know a man by the last name of Benjamin? He used to own a traveling hotel."

The assayer's face crinkled into a smile. "Sure, I know old Benjamin."

"Well, is he anywhere near here? My father's his partner."

"Six weeks ago Benjamin was working on a claim a half day's ride over the next ridge of hills."

"What direction would that be?" came from Jess.

The assayer pointed over his shoulder. "That way. Due east. There's a pass through the hills. It's easy riding."

"That don't matter," came from Jess. "We've ridden all the way from Switzer Wells."

"Do tell!" The assayer sounded admiring.

I thanked him for the information and left with Jess. My hopes were up again. We came up to Mahkto, who had never got down from his horse, and pointed to the east. He knew what I meant. He reined the gray around and started off in that direction without my having to say a word.

By crumbs, that's where we found them, Mr. Benjamin and Papa, that same afternoon, beside a little stream, shoveling dirt into the same kind of long wooden box. I wasn't sure that it was them at first, though another miner in this smaller valley over the hills from the assay office had told me they were "at home" on their claim. The two of them looked like gold miners—not someone's father or husband at all. They had untrimmed bushy beards and red-checkered shirts, Levis, and high, black boots.

So I wouldn't make a mistake in calling the wrong man "Papa" and perhaps insulting him, I took off my hat, which was really Cousin Jonah's big black one, to let myself be seen and yelled, "It's me, Damaris Boyd of Saint Louis, Missouri!"

"*Damaris!*" The black-bearded man, the taller one, dropped his shovel and came running toward me.

I started to cry. I was dog tired, and I was sore all over from riding for days. And I was happy. Any one of those reasons was good enough for crying. When Papa hauled me out of the saddle and held me against his chest, I cried harder than ever.

Finally, after I had dried my eyes and nose on his shirt, because I'd forgotten to bring a handkerchief, I answered the question he'd asked over and over again, "What in the name of God are you doing here, Damaris?"

I still had my arms around him, when I said, "I've come to bring you home."

"But I was going back to Missouri next month as soon as I went to visit Owen and saw my land."

I took my arms away from him. What he'd just said

really made me mad. Aunt Willa was absolutely right! Getting mad and doing something about it was good for ladies at times. I stopped crying right away. I told him, "We've seen Boyd Valley, and there's nothing there but grass and water. No, we're not in Missouri. We're out here, all of us. We're in Switzer Wells waiting for you. We didn't give up the ship, none of us. But Mama needs you!"

By now Jess had dismounted too and led her horse up to us. I introduced her, "Papa, this is Jessica King. She's from Switzer Wells too. And the Indian boy is Mahkto. He lives with us."

Mr. Benjamin, still carrying his shovel, came up to us. "By all that's holy, Charlie, it is the little girl on the train. It's your daughter in the flesh." He looked as if he couldn't believe his eyes and didn't truly want to.

I didn't answer him, the old whelp. He'd got us in all the trouble in the first place. It wasn't right that he and Papa should look so fit and Mama so poorly. I was sure she was working harder than they were, though Papa had arm muscles now.

My words were for Papa. "Mama, Ann Viola, William, and I are in Switzer Wells, and so is Cousin Jonah."

"Jonah, too?" Papa sounded amazed. "Where is Owen?"

"In Boyd Valley. He's the reason why we have the Apaches living with us."

Papa drew me over to a sawed-off log they must have used as a seat when they got tired of shoveling. He set me down on it. "Didn't you get my letter and the nugget?"

"Yes, but that was a long time ago. Too long."

"But, Damaris, I told your mother to *return* to Saint Louis."

"We didn't. We were already set up in business."

"In *business*? You and your brother and sister and mother?"

Jess started to laugh. She broke in from behind me, "They sure are, Mr. Boyd. And your relatives, too."

"My relatives? You mean Jonah?"

I nodded. "Yes, Jonah and Aunt Willa and Aunt Lily."

"Ye Gods and little fishes," Papa said softly. "Are *they* out here, too?"

"Not anymore, except for Jonah. Aunt Willa's back in Missouri, and Aunt Lily is in California. It's because they came and left that I've come here to bring you back with me before Mama collapses from working too hard."

"What is she working at?" Papa was shaking his head, as if he thought I was making it all up. My, but he needed a haircut!

Jess told him, laughing again, "Running a gold mine, Mr. Boyd."

Mr. Benjamin asked sharply, "A gold mine? That sweet little lady I saw on the train?"

"Yes, sir." I gave him what I hoped was a killing look. I knew what he was thinking: that we had a real gold mine and Mama was shoveling dirt into a flume too. I told him, "You should know about it. It used to belong to you."

"*To me?*" He still didn't understand.

"Yes, it's your traveling hotel, Mr. Benjamin. We put it up in Switzer Wells, because we knew that the railroad was going through there to Semple. Your hotel's right across the street from Jessica's family's hotel, isn't it, Jessica?" Aha, he'd expected me to sell it. I had kerflummoxed Mr. B. Benjamin all right.

"You bet the Nomad is. We serve whiskey and beer and the Nomad don't, but my pa says we're both making money hand over fist. We've both got more business than we can rightly handle."

I added, "And we can't find anybody to hire to help us out at the Nomad."

While Mahkto held the reins of the three horses and the burro, I told Papa and his partner about Owen and Natalie, the Apache band, and no house for us in Boyd Valley, about Mr. Ponder and Arthur, Mr. Toy, Cousin Jonah, and Mahkto. But I didn't say right then why Aunt Willa and Aunt Lily hadn't stayed or about what a disgraceful business Aunt Willa was engaged in back home. That could come later on. It wasn't the sort of thing to say in front of Mr. Benjamin. That old hyena of a man might laugh.

I finished with, "So we have to have help fast. Mama's really taking the tincture of lavender these days."

Jess put in, "Uh-huh, men drink whiskey. Ladies take tinctures. My pa knows!"

My Lord! Alcohol after all in the Nomad! I wondered if Mama knew. She said the tincture tasted terrible, even if it smelled heavenly.

Papa looked alarmed, as well he might be. He sat down on the stump beside me as if he was weary all of a sudden. "All right, Damaris, I'll go back with you. We'll start in the morning. You kids look to me as if you need a night of rest."

"So do the horses," I told Papa. "They could use some grass, too. There's plenty of it here."

Mahkto had got tired of standing around while I told our tale of woe to Papa and Mr. Benjamin. He'd taken the horses to the stream to drink.

Mr. Benjamin spoke up. "Come on, girls. We've got a pretty comfortable tent up there in the trees. You can have our bunks. Tonight I'll cook you up a venison stew that will stick to your ribs."

I got up and walked with Jess and him and Papa to a good-sized tent that I hadn't seen at first because of the trees around it.

As Mr. Benjamin walked beside me, he said, "You say that old white elephant of a hotel of mine is really doing a good business, huh?"

"It surely is. It isn't a get-rich-quick gold mine,

though. We work hard. We run our feet off in it."
I couldn't help but ask him, "How are you two doing
out here?"

"It could be better." Benjamin had taken a cheroot
out of his shirt pocket, lit it, and was now chewing
on its end. I could tell that he was regretting giving
the Nomad to me out of a guilty conscience or to get
rid of it because he wanted to run away from it. Well,
it was mine now. He hadn't wanted it. I'd been the
one to go along with Mr. Ponder and Aunt Willa to
make a go of it. Mr. Benjamin was stewing sweetly in
his own juices. He eyed me from under the brim of
his hat. "So you've made a tidy profit out of my old
place."

"Yes, we all have, Mr. Benjamin."

"Who's the manager, might I ask?"

"I am, Mr. Benjamin. I'm the desk clerk, too." I
plunked down on Papa's bunk, which was almost as
hard as the ground and only a little bit less hard than
Sable Satan's saddle had been.

"You are?" Papa couldn't believe this either, and
I saw how startled Mr. Benjamin was looking.

"Yes, I am. Aunt Willa taught me how because she
was the manager at first. Mama's the chambermaid
and laundry lady. Cousin Jonah's the waiter." Then
I told what everyone did around the hotel.

"But why are *you* the manager, Damaris?" I guessed
that Papa thought Cousin Jonah ought to be.

I said, "Because *I* decided who was going to be the

manager. The Nomad belongs to me. Free and clear, and Mama will back me up in whatever I decide to do. If she signs a paper about the Nomad it'll be legal, I guess. But the hotel's really mine, and Mama knows it!"

In spite of my weariness I grinned at Mr. Benjamin. "It's going just fine except for Mama working too hard. I've got the whole place set up properly. We even have tablecloths and china dishes."

Benjamin muttered to Papa, "I wish I had it back."

"Mama wishes you did, too, Mr. Benjamin," I told him, being honest.

Papa sighed as Jess lay down on Mr. Benjamin's bunk across from me. I supposed Mahkto had found someplace to curl up. He would never share our tent anywhere we camped. I didn't know if it was because we were white people or because we were girls.

My father told me as he and Benjamin went out, "Try to get some sleep before supper, honey."

I didn't fall asleep right away. I lay there listening to Jess's breathing, thinking. I'd been right in what I had said to Mr. Benjamin about Mama's wanting to leave the hotel business.

Mr. Benjamin's venison stew was even better than Mr. Toy's, though Benjamin's was cooked over a campfire in an iron pot, not on a stove. He'd made sourdough biscuits on a sheet of tin set in the coals. Mahkto ate with us and said "Okay" while he chased

the last of the gravy around his tin plate with a biscuit just the way the rest of us did.

All through supper Mr. Benjamin talked about the
Nomad and the interesting things that had happened
in it. Two outlaws had been shot to death in the dining room in one town. A cougar had walked through
the lobby and hall and out into the woods behind the
hotel in another. Three babies had been born in it,
and several worn-out old people had died there. Once
a tipped-over kerosene lamp had burned half of the
hotel down, and he'd had to get new boards and more
canvas.

He asked me, "Have you had any adventures
with it?"

"Not like those." I doubted if he'd understand all
the love troubles Mr. Ponder had had, so I kept quiet.
Mr. Benjamin, by his own admission, was a lifelong
bachelor. I figured by being one he'd saved some lady
from a lot of sorrow and grief.

After supper I asked Papa, "Did you earn that five
hundred dollars you lost on the train out here in the
goldfields?"

His eyes looked sheepish. They should have. I
didn't even look at Mr. Benjamin. Papa told me,
"I've got four hundred dollars of it. That should take
me to visit Owen and from there back to Saint Louis
in some style. I've got a horse."

I'd seen that he had. A horse and some blankets,
a few clothes, picks and shovels, a coffeepot, pots and

pans and tin plates and tin cutlery. That's all they seemed to have. But four hundred dollars was something—a very nice something!

"It's share and share alike with us. We're partners, you know," came from Mr. Benjamin.

"Then you have four hundred dollars too?" I asked the old whelp.

"That's right, little lady. We struck pay dirt for a while, but that was quite a time back." All at once, as if he tried to surprise me, he asked me, "Are you willing perchance to sell the Nomad back to me for four hundred dollars?"

Oh, he was a businessman all right. He knew that I wouldn't give it back to him. Maybe he'd given it to me out of feelings of guilt. Well, I surely didn't have any such foolish feelings toward him. I shook my head. "No, sir. It's worth more than that where it is in Switzer Wells. Remember, we had to buy the land to put it on, and we had to buy things to outfit it, and I've had to pay wages to my help. I figure it's worth about six hundred dollars as it stands right now."

He said, "You do have a business head, Miss Boyd." Then he added, "I wish you were a man and you played poker. You ought to be a worthy opponent." He looked quite wistful, I thought. He knew from experience what kind of player Papa was. There couldn't have been much of a challenge in playing with him.

I felt rather kindly toward Mr. Benjamin at that

moment. He wasn't calling me "little girl" any longer. I liked that. It had been high time for him to get back to "Miss Boyd," the address he'd used on the note he'd sent me on the train. Oh, I knew what Papa would say, but all the same I made up my mind. First, I took a deep breath, and then I said, "All right, sir, I want to put a proposition to you. How about putting up six hundred dollars against my hotel in a game of chance?" I knew from Mr. Ponder's lessons that this was a very polite way of saying "poker." By my putting it this way, Benjamin also realized that I knew how to play the game. I was being fair. I wasn't being guilty of get-rich-quick, and after all Mr. Benjamin was the one who had put the poker idea into my head.

"Damaris!" Papa exploded the way I had guessed he would. Like a firecracker on the Glorious Fourth back home. "No one in our family plays poker!" Well, that was good news from him. He had learned something out in Arizona Territory. Maybe Mr. Benjamin had poker on his mind, because Papa wouldn't play at all with him anymore.

I comforted Papa with, "I don't mean for you to play. I'm going to do the playing, and just to keep the game honest, I want all of you to watch it."

Mr. Benjamin chuckled. He was delighted, the old hyena. He asked, "Are you in the habit of cheating at cards, Miss Boyd?" By crumbs, he was accepting my offer.

I smiled at him. "No, sir, I am not. Do you have a deck of cards?"

"That I do." He went into the tent and came back in a moment with the dirtiest, most dog-eared deck of cards I'd ever seen. They should have been washed with soap and water, but then so should every one of us.

I asked as politely as I could, "Mr. Benjamin, you said you had four hundred dollars that you made mining. Do you really have six hundred dollars? That's my price, not a penny less than that." I hoped he wouldn't try to make up the two hundred dollars in merchandise or in gold nuggets, though I knew that the assayer over the hills would tell me what nuggets would be worth.

Mr. Benjamin didn't seem offended at my asking. He said, "Well, not exactly in cash, Miss Boyd. But I'll give you an I.O.U. for the other two hundred dollars, if you win. How does that strike you?"

I hesitated, looking at him, then at Papa, who was looking upset. But Jess nodded her head. She knew about scoundrels from all the novels she'd read, and she seemed to think he was honest.

I decided to trust him. I said, "Let's play."

"Damaris, I forbid this," Papa fumed.

"Papa, you can't forbid it." I was being very patient with him. "The Nomad belongs to me. I've made up my mind."

And so I had. Of course, I'd like to get Mr. Benjamin's money and keep the Nomad, too, but there was Mama to think about. Yes, for her sake I was willing to lose the hotel. It wasn't as if I'd be losing everything. After all, I had some profits from the place and Papa's four hundred dollars. Put together, the money would make a nice sum to take home with us as a memento of our trip to Arizona Territory even after I'd paid out wages at the end of the month.

By crumbs, Uncle Owen wasn't going to get a penny of this money either. When he talked to Papa in Boyd Valley, I planned to stick as close to Papa as a mustard plaster so I could tell Owen Boyd no myself. Papa could weaken but not me.

Papa gave up protesting, when I said, "Trust me, please. After all, I found you way out here, didn't I? I know what I'm doing."

I ignored Mr. Benjamin's chuckling. His opinions really didn't matter to me anymore, though his money did. He was shuffling the cards on top of the cut-off stump I'd sat on that morning. It was their dining table as well as a seat. He asked me, "What kind of game do you suggest?"

I told him, "Showdown poker, Mr. Benjamin." That game was fast, and it didn't require one bit of bluffing. I was sure that Mr. Benjamin, who doted on poker, was a very fine bluffer. He'd probably kerflummoxed Papa on the train by bluffing. That wouldn't work with me.

"Well, well, Miss Boyd," was all he said, but his

eyebrows rose. It seemed to me that he was looking at me with new respect. He knew that I was refusing to bluff. He knew I was choosing my own ground. He'd learned from me already that all folks from Saint Louis were not to be taken in by his wiles.

I reached for the cards. "I'll deal the cards, Mr. Benjamin."

But when he gave them to me, I handed them to Jess to shuffle. I trusted her. Mr. Benjamin gave me a strange grin. Oh, I doubted if he would truly have trusted me to shuffle them either. He knew his oats all right when it came to card games. Well, thanks to Mr. Ponder, so did I. Wherever Mr. Ponder was at the moment, I forgave him for eloping with Mrs. Dooley. I wished him and Belinda Ponder well.

Jess shuffled the deck in such a clumsy way that anybody could tell she wasn't a card player and had to be honest. Then she handed the cards back to me.

I acted very lighthearted about the game to show Mr. Benjamin that I knew my poker onions. I dealt fast. I wanted to win but wouldn't waste away of sorrow if I lost because of helping Mama. Too, I wanted to get the game over fast, another reason for choosing showdown poker.

The first card I turned went face up to Mr. Benjamin's side of the stump. It was a two of diamonds, so dirty that Jess had to bring the kerosene lamp closer to the stump so we could make it out.

The next card I turned up came to me. It was a

jack of clubs. Because it outranked a two of anything, I was ahead in the game. But the game had only started.

The third card, which went to Mr. Benjamin, was an ace of clubs. That put him high card in the game. He was ahead—winning. My heart sank a bit.

My card, the fourth, was a three of clubs. He was still ahead.

The next card, the fifth, was his. It was a king of hearts, frowning at him the way all kings did. He was still ahead. He had two important cards. I was naturally worried but was very careful not to show it in front of him and Papa and Jess. No one should ever look worried in a poker game, according to Mr. Ponder. So I kept a calm look on my face.

Card number six came to me, a little one, a four of clubs.

Everybody, except Mahkto, who wasn't one bit interested in poker and who had gone to see to the horses and burro, sucked in his breath excitedly as I dealt the seventh card to Mr. Benjamin. It was a two of clubs.

By the look on the old whelp's whiskery face, he liked that card. It gave him a pair of two's, the two of diamonds, the first card I'd dealt him, and the two of clubs. My heart sank some more—to my ankles at least.

The eighth card, which came to my side of the stump, was a six of hearts.

The ninth card of the ten cards in all that I'd be dealing in the game of showdown poker was an eight of spades. It went to him. It didn't fit in with a flush, but he still had that pair of two's unless I drew a three or a four or a six or jack of something, he was bound to win the game. I scented that I was very soon going out of the hotel business, but I didn't even let out a sigh. Mr. Ponder would not have approved if I had.

An owl hooted in the trees before I turned up the final card on the stump top. My card again this time. It positively grinned up into my face, even though its head was turned sideways. It was the jack of hearts.

By crumbs, I'd won! I'd beaten him. I'd come to glory. I'd made up for Papa's disgrace. I had two jacks to his pair of two's. The Nomad was still mine, but so was Mr. Benjamin's four hundred dollars and his I.O.U. for two hundred dollars more. We'd be going home in high style to Missouri, it seemed to me.

As Mr. Benjamin collected the cards, he told me rather sadly, "Well, Miss Boyd, you won fair and square. It appears to me as if you own everything now." He laughed sharply. "How about giving a poor old man a job in your establishment now that it seems I'm also going to lose my partner on this claim?"

By the time he'd finished speaking, I had another idea. Thinking fast, I told him, "Mr. Benjamin, I'll do better than that. I'll give you my establishment if you'll agree to what I ask."

He shot me a very suspicious glance. "What would that be? An arm and a leg? Or do you want a smart partner in the Nomad?"

I laughed. He still had some of the ways of a hyena. Here he was offering himself as a partner, though he wasn't even going to put any money into the hotel the way Mr. Ponder and Aunt Willa had. Like Mama, I doubted if Mr. Benjamin would ever walk the streets of New Jerusalem. I told him, "No, I don't want any more partners. I've already had two of them. What would you say if I offered to give the hotel back to you if you write me another I.O.U.?"

He bit like a bass but managed to be cautious at the same time. "How much is it to be this time, Miss Boyd?" he wanted to know.

"Five hundred dollars, that's all I want."

"That's a lot of money," he told me, sounding sour.

"I'm not asking for it right this minute. It can be sent to me later in Saint Louis when you've made that much profit from the hotel. How about that?"

He wasn't smiling when he asked me, "Do you trust me to send it to you?" He was eyeing me quite strangely.

I said, "Well, to tell the truth, Mr. Benjamin, there is a bit more to the proposition."

I heard Papa let out his breath in a sort of sigh.

Mr. Benjamin didn't pay him any heed. He kept his eyes on me. "All right, Miss Boyd, what would it be?"

"You'll have to keep Mr. Toy, the cook, and the
two Apaches, Arthur and Mahkto, as long as they
want to stay. You can't turn them out homeless. And
you have to give free room and board to the schoolteacher, Mr. Wroth, and keep Cousin Jonah on as
long as he wants to stay once we're gone." I added,
"Of course, Jonah is a Boyd. He'll keep an eye on
things for me and telegraph me if anything doesn't
work out just right in the hotel."

Mr. Benjamin grunted. "I see." Then he went on
to say, "I'll bet you know the uses of the telegraph all
right."

"Yes, sir, I've sent off quite a few telegrams, and
I've got results from them too." In my opinion the
telegraph was a marvelous modern instrument.

All at once Benjamin said, "All right, I'll take over
the Nomad on an I.O.U., a promissory note, and
when I've made the five hundred dollars, I'll send the
money to you by messenger in Saint Louis. I'll be riding to Switzer Wells with you tomorrow then."

I held out my hand to him to seal our agreement
with a handshake. After a moment he took it, but
first he said to Jess and Papa, "You heard every word
this little terror on two feet just said, didn't you? I
want witnesses to everything we've said tonight. I just
wish I had it all down in writing."

After they had nodded, I told him, "Mr. Benjamin,
I'm as honest as the day is long."

Still holding my hand, he said, "I hope to heaven you stay that way."

I gave out a sigh of satisfaction. I'd done it. I felt on top of the world. Papa was beaming at me with pride or perhaps it was amazement.

I beamed back at him.

He said, "Damaris, you astonish me at all you've learned out here."

That was true enough. I had. I had a business head, but I wasn't a female outlaw or heartless, and I didn't ever intend to be.

All the same Papa didn't know why I was still smiling fondly at him. It wasn't just because of the compliment he'd given me. He had some more surprises coming!

Aunt Willa was going to have plenty to say to him about his character and Uncle Owen's. But the biggest surprise of all would come from Mama, who had changed from the lady he'd brought out to Arizona Territory. She might be weary, but the sight of him would revive her spirits. I was pretty sure it would also warm up her tongue.

I said, "Papa, I can just hear the things in my mind that Mama will have to say to you."

One thing about Arizona Territory—maybe men went wild in it, but women didn't. They seemed to get stronger in the character, if not in the body.

I'd bet anything we'd be on our way to Missouri in

less than ten days' time. If I knew Mama, by crumbs, we would be on the train!

And the first thing I planned to do back in Saint Louis was to have a little chat with Aunt Willa about Mrs. Dooley. That had been my idea of a dirty trick. Aunt Willa had no right to make money off us at a distance. It had been all right with me when she was in Switzer Wells, but not when she was in Saint Louis. Old as she was and a business lady, too, I intended to say a thing or two to her.

By crumbs, I certainly did intend to!

AUTHOR'S NOTE

Although this novel is fiction, there is a goodly amount of factual material included that might be of interest to readers.

It was not at all unheard of for ships and trains to empty of almost all male passengers when they were in the vicinity of a gold strike. During the 1849 California gold rush, for instance, ships were abandoned in San Francisco by their crews who headed for the diggings.

"Gold fever," though not a clinical disease, is a very real thing, as American history proves over and over again. It is the lure of get-rich-quick that seems to keep gold (silver, uranium) seekers going. Some men have sought gold all their lives and still are prospecting as very old men without ever having struck it rich.

My material about trains is factual. There were very luxurious Pullman cars and dining cars in 1882 and remarkably fancy menus, the result of canned foods and of cars filled with ice. By treaty provisions, peaceful Indians were allowed to ride trains free of charge.

Several words I've used might make readers wonder. One of these is *okay*. It was in use as early as 1840 in that spelling. *Telegram* seems very modern, too, but it was in common use in 1882. The expression, "by crumbs," was current slang. So were the words *daisy, dumpling, old whelp,* and many others I've used.

The names of the songs mentioned were 1882 tunes, and the titles of Aunt Lily's romances and Jess King's dime novels were real titles of the day. The action-filled dime novel, which sometimes sold for five cents, was very popular reading material (it could scarcely be called literature) from 1860 to 1920. I have read a number of them preparing for this novel. Quite a few of Jess King's overblown sentences are direct quotes from dime novels published in the early 1880's. Thousands of dime novels were printed, many of them as series. Deadwood Dick, Railroad Rob, and Fred Fear-Not were fictional heroes. Actual people, such as Calamity Jane, Wild Bill Hickok, Buffalo Bill, and the outlaw brothers, Frank and Jesse James, figured as characters in other lurid dime novels. (Jesse James, the Missouri bandit, did in fact die in April, 1882.)

Spar City, Leacock, Switzer Wells, and Semple are

not real towns, but they are based on some communities that once were—and still are.

The very unusual Christmas tree I've described existed with its glorious decorations of cigars, whiskey bottles in various stages of emptiness, and dynamite sticks.

As for photography, it had come a goodly distance from the daguerreotype in 1882. Small cameras with plates of gelatin were in use by then. Camera film was "just around the corner" at the time of this novel, so my Mr. Gibson must still struggle with heavy plates.

What I've said about Apache Indians is fact. Apache bands sometimes did hold child captives who were white. Most Indian tribes, because of their very high infant death rate, greatly valued children—all children. White captives were raised as Indians. Quite often when the children were reunited with their real families, they longed to be back with the Indians. (Indian children were rarely punished, something that could not be said about nineteenth-century white children.) It would not be out of character for my Natalie Boyd, though she marries a white man and has been to school, to live with her Apache "relatives" by preference. I do not pretend to be an authority on the Apache idea of kinship, which is very complex, but from what I gather, nearly every Apache in a band is a "cousin" to every other Apache.

One old Apache taboo is the eating of fish, though wood rats and mule are considered a delicacy. Apache custom in the nineteenth century forbid a man to speak to the girl he was courting and, after marriage, to his mother-in-law. He "purchased" his bride from her parents by a gift of horses. The more beautiful and more desirable the girl, the more horses the suitor gave.

Camels could be found straying in the Southwestern deserts in 1882. Earlier they had been used as transport beasts by the U.S. Army, found to be unsuitable, and therefore turned loose.

What I have written about lizards is true. My daughter Alexandra, who plucked a large alligator lizard off a stucco wall some years ago to put in a terrarium, can testify to their ability to bite. And I have swept "alive" but disconnected lizard tails out of my garage and study more than once when wandering lizards have invaded and surprised.

I suspect that some readers will refuse to accept the idea of a collapsible hotel touring the West on a railroad flatcar. Well, there was such a hotel! And it went from place to place in just that fashion. It was called the Wandering Hotel and catered to railroad construction crews. My Nomad is based on it. I don't know if tin plates were nailed to the tables in the Wandering Hotel. I do know, however, that such a expedient was used in some very busy restaurants of the Old West. Travelers commented in horror at the practice!

In writing this book, I've used a number of sources. Some of them are: *History of Arizona* (4 volumes), by Ward R. Adams; *This Is the Desert,* by Phil Ault; *Ghosts of Adobe Walls,* by Nell Murbarger; *Arizona Sketches,* by Joseph A. Munk; and the *Arizona Writer's Program,* a valuable collection of material by Arizona writers.

Sources dealing with methods of transportation of the period are: *The Railroaders,* by Keith Wheeler; *The Pacific Tourist,* edited by Frederick E. Shearer; and *American Horse-Drawn Vehicles,* by Jack D. Rittenhouse.

My material on Apaches came chiefly from: *Apache Land,* by Ross Santee, and *I Fought with Geronimo,* by Jason Betzinez (an Apache), written with W. S. Nye.

My source on photography is *Photography and the American Scene,* by Robert Taft.

A most interesting and entertaining little book, which I can recommend to anyone at all interested in the history of the West is *A Room for the Night,* by Richard A. Van Orman. It deals with old hotels.

And, of course, I also recommend the book I refer to throughout this novel. It is the *Ladies' Indispensable Assistant, Being a Companion for the Sister, Mother and Wife,* published in New York in 1852. This guide to just about everything under the sun a proper lady should know seemingly has an anonymous author, but her fame, whoever she was, lives. The book exists in a modern reprint edition.

Three librarians deserve my thanks for various odd bits of information I requested from them. They are Marie Genung, Library, University of California, Riverside; Juleanne Good of the Saint Louis Public Library, Saint Louis, Missouri; and Colonel A. Stevenson of the Riverside Public Library, Riverside, California. I wish also to thank pharmacist William Honeyman for information regarding the alcoholic content of old-time tinctures and my late husband, John Louis Beatty, for all of the technical information about the game of poker. (The specific game of showdown Damaris Boyd plays with Mr. Benjamin was played by the two of us first and then incorporated into the novel because by accident it turned out to be a suspenseful series of cards.)

Patricia Beatty
January, 1975

Now a resident of Southern California, Patricia Beatty was born in Portland, Oregon. She was graduated from Reed College there, and then taught high-school English and history for four years. Later she held various positions as science and technical librarian. Recently she taught Writing Fiction for Children in the Extension Department of the University of California, Los Angeles. She has had a number of historical novels published by Morrow, several of them dealing with the American West in the 1860 to 1895 period.

Mrs. Beatty has lived in Coeur d'Alene, Idaho; London, England; and Wilmington, Delaware; as well as on the West Coast. She and her late husband, Dr. John Beatty, co-authored a number of books. One of them, *The Royal Dirk*, was chosen as an Award book by the Southern California Council on Children's and Young People's Literature.